P9-DLZ-239

"I gotta move. You need to go home."

"That's not happening," he insisted. "People want you dead, but I'm not one of them. You have to trust someone before it's too late, Min."

Anger spiraled low in her belly. "Gosh, you mean like when I trusted you last year? Thanks, but no thanks, Jacobs. I hereby free you of any guilt or misguided duty you feel necessary to save me from my enemies. They're my problem. Not yours."

"Wrong. They were our problem then, and they are our problem now."

"If they were our problem then, why did you abandon me?" she asked.

"I didn't abandon you."

"It doesn't matter right now. This is my battle. Go home. My life has been over since I first stepped foot in that house in Red Rye. I was a dead woman walking and didn't even know it. Now, I know it. You'd be better off walking away now with your life."

GOING ROGUE IN RED RYE COUNTY

KATIE METTNER

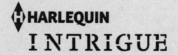

If you purchased this book without a cover you should be aware
that this book is stolen property. It was reported as "unsold and
destroyed" to the publisher, and neither the author nor the
publisher has received any payment for this "stripped book."

To my husband.

For picking me up when I fall, dusting me off and reminding me
that the stories I tell matter. Your unwavering faith in me is the
reason this book exists. I love you.

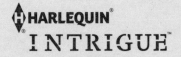

INTRIGUE

ISBN-13: 978-1-335-58251-5

Recycling programs
for this product may
not exist in your area.

Going Rogue in Red Rye County

Copyright © 2023 by Katie Mettner

All rights reserved. No part of this book may be used or reproduced in
any manner whatsoever without written permission except in the case of
brief quotations embodied in critical articles and reviews.

This is a work of fiction. Names, characters, places and incidents
are either the product of the author's imagination or are used fictitiously.
Any resemblance to actual persons, living or dead, businesses,
companies, events or locales is entirely coincidental.

For questions and comments about the quality of this book,
please contact us at CustomerService@Harlequin.com.

Harlequin Enterprises ULC
22 Adelaide St. West, 41st Floor
Toronto, Ontario M5H 4E3, Canada
www.Harlequin.com

Printed in U.S.A.

Katie Mettner wears the title of "the only person to lose her leg after falling down the bunny hill" and loves decorating her prosthetic leg to fit the season. She lives in Northern Wisconsin with her own happily-ever-after and wishes for a dog, now that her children are grown. Katie has an addiction to coffee and Twitter and a lessening aversion to Pinterest—now that she's quit trying to make the things she pins.

Books by Katie Mettner

Harlequin Intrigue

Secure One

Going Rogue in Red Rye County

CAST OF CHARACTERS

FBI Special Agent Wilhelmina August—Mina is injured and on the run after an undercover job goes sideways. Her motto is Trust No One, and that includes her partner, Roman Jacobs.

FBI Special Agent Roman Jacobs—Roman has spent a year searching for his partner after she went missing from her hospital bed. He's determined to prove to her the botched rescue wasn't his fault or die trying.

The Madame—Known only by her moniker, she is building an empire on the backs of vulnerable women. She rules with an iron fist, and every woman in the Red Rye house fears her, including Mina.

The Miss—As second-in-command, she follows The Madame's orders to a T. Or does she?

Marlise—Bought by The Madame, but holds an alliance with Mina. If the FBI wants her to talk, they'd better find her friend.

Special Agent in Charge David Moore—He assigned Mina the undercover job then failed to protect her. He'll stop at nothing to get his agent back alive.

Cal Newfellow—Roman's foster brother and owner of Secure One Security. As a mercenary turned businessman, there isn't much Cal can't do or obtain. Roman trusts him, but should Mina?

Chapter One

Mina stole the gun from the safe while he slept. Smith & Wesson. A .38 revolver. Small. Point-and-shoot. That was all that mattered when she tucked it under her waistband. She patted the inside of the safe, pleased to find extra rounds and a stack of hundreds Nathan had been saving for a rainy day. Someday, she'd make it right, but for now, she'd have to owe him one. Hell, if it helped her get out of this alive, she might owe him her life.

On her way to the front door, Mina paused and pulled the curtain back from the living-room window. Dim headlights swept across the lawn as an old pickup truck swung around the corner. She ducked her head back. That was the third time she'd seen the same battered pickup since dinner. It was trying too hard to fit in here in Chester. Her trained eye said it stuck out like a sore thumb. Mina had to wonder how long it had been casing the place. She didn't know, but its appearance told her one thing—time was running out. Correction. Her time had run out.

Another peek out the window showed her neighbors having a party on their front porch, and while they'd be good noise cover, if they spotted her, they'd tell the person driving the truck exactly when she'd left and what direction she'd headed. She couldn't let that happen. Her only escape was out the back, where she had her route planned through the trees, if she wanted to avoid the road and whoever was in that truck.

She bit back a strangled snort as she plastered herself against the outside wall of the laundry room. As if she didn't know who was in that truck. She knew, and they weren't Boy Scouts. Maybe she should say they weren't Girl Scouts. Nah, there was no way The Madame would send girls. The Madame would send thugs who she knew without a shadow of a doubt Mina couldn't beat.

She'd have to go it on foot for now. She paused for a moment to make sure Nathan hadn't awakened. Fat chance of that happening considering how many sleeping pills she'd dumped in his beer the second time she saw that truck in the neighborhood. Guilt lanced through her, but she didn't have time to dwell on it, so she grabbed her go-bag from the laundry room, slung it over her shoulders and grasped the walking pole waiting at the door. It was now or never. Her heart pounded, and the blood rushed through her veins at the idea of stepping out into the open. She had twenty feet of open space to clear before she'd meet the tree line. Twenty feet was nothing if you could run, but it was an eternity when you couldn't. And Mina couldn't. She could barely walk and was held up by nothing more than a carbon fiber leg brace, the sturdy walking pole and a lot of determination.

A glance through the curtain on the back door and a deep breath in gave her the strength to turn the doorknob and step out to the concrete steps. She paused and picked her way down the steps carefully. Falling this early in the game was a guaranteed death sentence. She took her time, but when her feet hit the grass, she dug the pole in for all she was worth and half ran, half limped toward the trees. Those trees were the reason she rented a room here. The long oak fence on each side of the property blocking the neighbors' view helped too. It gave her cover to her surefire escape route. Surefire if the men looking for her didn't know about it, that is.

She hesitated on her next step. Did the men who were after her know about the woods? She couldn't say for sure, but she would have to assume they did. All of that said, her choices were limited. The street left her wide open to the people in the truck. At least the woods gave her cover, and she knew them better than anyone. She'd mapped out multiple escape routes through the underbrush—routes others wouldn't know existed. If they tried to follow, she'd hear them crashing through the underbrush, and that would give her time to change direction.

Finally swallowed up by the dark branches of the trees, Mina let out half the breath she'd been holding.

She quickly found the first stash of supplies she'd tucked under a tree for an emergency. She knelt, but old habits kicked in, and she glanced up at the tree canopy. She'd lucked out. The stars were hidden behind heavy clouds, giving her a chance to escape unseen. The weather could buy her hours. Hours she'd need to get out of this one-horse town. It wasn't going to be easy, and she knew it, but Mina had little choice in the matter now. The sands in her hourglass had run out much quicker than expected and left her questioning everything—including her roommate's allegiance to her.

Mina forced her mind to calm. "You've been trained to escape dangerous situations," she reminded herself as she shook out her shoulders. "You might be a little bit dented and rusty, but it's like riding a bike. Trust in yourself."

Her pep talk over, she felt around for the stash hidden inside the hollowed-out tree. Mina's backpack only held her personal items that wouldn't raise her roommate's suspicions should he check the bag. She always knew if she had to run for the trees, a different set of supplies would be needed to survive. She dropped her backpack and slipped her tactical chest pack on, immediately hiking the backpack over it and strapping it on. She moved the gun to its rightful spot on her hip and ran her hands over the chest pack, making sure everything was in place.

Binoculars, compass, spare burner phone, emergency shelter, knife, protein bars, water and maps of the topography of North Dakota. She was as ready as she'd ever be.

The walk to Bismarck was going to take a full three days, and that was if she could walk the required miles each day. Chances were good that wouldn't happen. Her foot had been getting worse instead of better, and it was going to make traveling through the woods nearly impossible. Regardless, she had to stay hidden as she worked her way toward the storage unit outside of Bismarck, where a car, a new name and a new life waited for her. That was how it had been for the last year. A new car, name and town every three months, no matter what. This time, she got lazy. When she made it two weeks past the three-month mark, she stayed. She was tired, and the safety she'd found in Chester gave her hope she could stay another few months, even if in the back of her mind she knew she was playing with fire. She just got burned. Hopefully, she had time to put out the flames before they got her for good.

Her back plastered against the tree, Mina took a calming breath and shook out her legs. "You got this, girl," she muttered to herself.

That had been Mina's mantra all her life until her injury. Now, a year later, she was still dealing with the fallout from it, and it was going to get worse before it got better. She would need every ounce of strength she had to survive.

"Clear your head," she chanted, her breath making little puffs of white in the cold October air. A deep breath in squared her shoulders naturally, and she pushed off into the darkened forest. It was time to move if she ever wanted to see the light of day again.

ROMAN PULLED THE rumbly truck over to the curb and put it in Park. He doused the dim headlights on the old truck, which had more rust than paint but was forgettable in a town like Chester, North Dakota. He had to be forgettable, for his partner's sake. Special Agent Wilhelmina August had been his partner for six years, and as far as he was concerned, she still was.

He eyed the neat-as-a-pin two-story home across the street from where he'd parked. He couldn't picture Mina August living there. At least not the Mina August he knew a year ago. The Mina August of today, he didn't know a thing about, and that was what drove him to this tiny town on a Sunday night.

Roman tipped his head side to side to force the negative thoughts away. He was here to make right what he'd done wrong, but first, he had to convince Mina he wasn't here to hurt her. That would be his biggest challenge, considering their last encounter. She was a federal agent, but she was also a scared woman who was alone, on the run and in pain. Guilt ripped through him as swiftly as wildfire. She was alone because he hadn't prepared for every scenario. She was running for her life because he hadn't mitigated the threat before it was too late. She was in pain because he failed to do his job. They both knew it, which was why Mina would shoot first and ask questions later. The phrase *trust no one* was ingrained in them at the academy, and Roman had no doubt Mina would trust him least of all.

Taking a few deep breaths, Roman calmed his mind and focused on the task at hand. Getting Mina somewhere safe. He climbed from the truck and approached a group of people sitting on a porch next door to Mina's rented room. He'd been driving around the block every thirty minutes, hoping to see her outside, but it hadn't happened. He could wait no longer. He'd thought about sneaking around the back of the house to see what was there, but with his luck, it would be a Doberman. He wasn't in the mood for a trip to the ER. He had tracked Mina to Chester after a full year of searching, and he wouldn't let her get away now.

"Hey, is Caitlyn around?" he asked, approaching the sidewalk with nonchalance. He just needed to confirm her location.

"There ain't no Caitlyn here, man," a dude said right before he spit a wad of chewing tobacco over the porch railing.

Classy. Roman fought hard against the eye roll threatening his composure.

"Shoot, she told me she was 1897 North Bradford Street," he answered, making a show of looking at the house number.

A woman hooked her thumb over her shoulder. "That's next door. This is 1895. A woman moved in there, but we don't know her name. Not super friendly. She rarely leaves the place. I'd go crazy my-self but to each their own." She took a long draw on her cigarette like it was life-giving oxygen.

"Oh, I'm sorry," Roman said, lacing his words with contriteness. "Well, here," he said, jogging up the sidewalk with a picture in his hand. "That's my friend Caitlyn. Does she look like the woman next door?"

"Sure does," said the dude before spitting more tobacco out the side of his lip.

Roman glanced to his right and shrugged. "House is dark, so she must be gone or sleeping. I'll stop by tomorrow. Thanks for the help." He raised his hand in a wave and jogged back to his truck. He rolled half-way down the street before he flipped the headlights on and rumbled out of the neighborhood. Something didn't feel right. If Roman had learned one thing after the fiasco in Red Rye, it was to follow his gut. His gut told him to turn left and make one last pass around the property.

He'd gotten confirmation that Mina lived there, but there was no point knocking on the door when it was buttoned up tight and no lights were on. With the neighbors outside, he couldn't sneak into the back-yard either. Roman knew her as well as he knew him-self, and if she noticed his truck circling the house, she'd be gone. Tomorrow he'd knock on the door, and she'd either be there or she wouldn't, but at least in the daylight, he might avoid getting shot. The deep bass of his laughter filled the truck.

"As if, man. The first thing she's going to do when she sees you darken her doorstep is shoot. She won't even bother asking questions."

Probably true and rightly so. As far as his partner was concerned, he'd let her down, and while she didn't know the whole story, the part she did know looked damning. He wasn't the guy she thought he was, and that bothered him. He'd spent the past year looking for her just to prove he wasn't heartless enough to let her get hurt on purpose. Or worse yet, that he was working for The Madame. If she believed he was the reason the operation went sideways, he'd never get within ten feet of her. The guilt raging through him forced a grunt from his lips. They'd been partners for six years, and he prayed Mina knew he'd never compromise an operation for his own gain.

Darkness had fallen since the last time he'd turned down the old dirt road that made up the back half of the property Mina rented. It wasn't a block so much as it was three streets and a gravel road through the forest. It would make a perfect escape route, and he had no doubt that was why she'd rented that house. He tapped the brake and pulled the truck over to the side of the road before he doused the lights.

An escape route.

A fence protected the backyard on each side, and Roman would bet his shield the back door led directly to the tree line. She'd be prepared to run. He didn't even question the truth of that statement. The problem was, knowing what he knew, how was Mina going to go it on foot? She'd need a vehicle sooner rather than later. Roman disabled the dome light and slid out of the truck. He walked a bit until he'd lined himself up with the back of Mina's house.

Wait. No. She wouldn't do that. She'd work those trees to her advantage and cross the road somewhere else. She would walk this grove of trees halfway down the block, cross the dirt road in three steps and be back in the trees. That was what he'd do. Staying in the grass off the edge of the road, Roman searched for any sign of footprints. They wouldn't be solid proof she was on the run, but no one was going to be walking on this road in the rain for fun.

He walked another quarter of a mile before he noticed a tumble of gravel off the edge of the road. The heel depression told him it was manmade. Or, in this case, more likely made by a woman. He flicked his flashlight up onto the road and noticed three prints, the left one with a drag on the toe. The sole pattern, and the word *Vibram* stamped in the dirt, gave her away. Mina wore one specific brand of boots, and he'd spent enough time following her footprints to know the sole pattern intimately. He'd found his partner. Well, he found where she had been. Now, the search reset.

Roman shook his head as he pulled himself into his truck. He hadn't been this close to Mina in a year.

He wasn't going to let her slip through his fingers. A light mist was on his windshield when he got back inside the truck, and he ran the wipers. He had to find her before The Madame did. He'd spooked her, which he expected, but he couldn't let her get away. The night would be long, but if he could track her down, it would be worth it.

With the rain falling, he'd easily be able to follow her footprints through the woods, but he'd likely get shot before he could say his piece. Roman only saw one option. Find where the trees ended and be waiting for her there.

It was a chance he had to take.

Chapter Two

Why *wouldn't* it start raining? As if Mina didn't have enough to deal with as it was. Now she had to worry about staying dry. She had three shelters along her route that would provide resting spots, but she would have to cover her miles each day if she was going to utilize them. Since she had to bug out in the night, she wouldn't make the first shelter before dawn. That meant she would have to keep her eyes open for someplace she could hide during the daylight hours tomorrow.

She would go as fast as she could, but the rain was going to slow her down simply because her foot hated it. From what she'd read, that was common with an injury like hers. When your foot was shattered beyond repair, there wasn't much that would help the pain. Whenever it rained or snowed, Mina turned into a cranky old woman in need of a heating pad and some menthol rub. She didn't have either of those things out here, so she'd have to put it out of her mind and push on. Her life likely depended on it.

Mina had found the river quickly enough, but the

long hike through the trees in the dark was treacherous. Walking exposed out on the road wasn't an option, even if she wished it were. There were too many farms along these roads. There was too great a chance one of the farmers would remember the woman in a combat vest hoofing it down the highway with a heavy limp. Her only choice was to move about under the cover of darkness and trees.

She kept her head pointed down at the dim light strapped to her walking pole. It lit her path without lighting up the entire night. Traveling without it under the heavy canopy of trees was too dangerous, so it was a risk worth taking. There would be only so far that she could push her foot, and falling would only hurt her, literally and figuratively. If she could find a secure shelter, she could sit it out another night just to give herself a fighting chance at making it to Bismarck.

She'd spent the last two hours meticulously running the last four months of her life through her head. She analyzed every move she made, trying to determine which one had been the wrong one. She'd come up empty-handed. Mina was positive she hadn't left herself vulnerable to any outside forces. Nathan, her roommate, was the only one who had checked her out, and her story held, so it didn't make sense that The Madame had found her here. She checked her belongings for trackers and never found any, so how did they know where she was? She purposely didn't have a car to avoid being tracked or, more likely, blown to bits when she started it up one day.

Unless her breadcrumbs had finally paid off.

The thought jolted her, and she almost tripped on a log. She hesitated for a moment. Had he found her? She shook her head and forced her feet forward. She couldn't risk stopping on the off chance the person in the truck wasn't out to kill her. She had to get to her car.

She'd bought the car with cash and never registered it. There was no way anyone knew that Caitlyn Carver owned an old, beat-up blue Ford Fairlane. She chuckled, and the sound rose into the trees and fell back down upon her. To her ears, it wasn't amused. She'd spent countless hours locked inside a storage unit working on the car to ensure it would run when the time came. And the time always came. Mina was glad she'd pilfered that pair of plates off an old junker just last week. They were tucked securely in her backpack for when she arrived at the unit. They wouldn't get her far, but they didn't have to. Once she hit another big city, she'd disappear on public transportation, never to be seen again.

"Maybe that was my mistake," she muttered, stepping over a fallen tree. She nearly caught her toe on a branch but saved herself at the last second. With her heart pounding, she stopped and took a few deep breaths to settle it again. She also took a minute to check her map, so she'd know when she had to cross the next open area. The time was coming, and it would require her to cross a farmer's field that was wider than she'd like. If this were summer, she could hide in the corn, but it was almost November, and the corn had long since been picked.

Mina blew out a breath and dug her pole into the soil, the scent of wet earth drifting into her nostrils and sending her back to a time she'd prefer never to think about again, but those memories, they didn't care. They dragged her back to that night every chance they got. The smoke. The screaming. The terror she felt in her gut as a seasoned FBI agent when she realized she wasn't getting out alive. Never in her thirty-five years of life had she felt so utterly helpless as she had the night the flames closed in around her. The eyes. The eyes she recognized but couldn't place as she was dragged to a window, the new source of oxygen fueling the flames.

Her foot caught on a vine, and she pitched forward, running her forehead smack-dab into a fallen log. Mina fell to the ground and fought for air while a trickle of blood ran down her forehead. Once she could think clearly again, she made precise movements with every one of her extremities to ensure they worked before she pushed herself into a sitting position.

"Great," she mumbled, fumbling in her pack for a bandanna. She pulled it out, spun it around a couple of times and tied it around the bleeding gash on her head. At least what she assumed was a gash. It wasn't like she was at the Ritz and could just check the gilded mirror. "Sarcasm. Works every time." Mina chuckled and pushed herself to a standing position, then brushed off her clothes. She checked the ground for anything that may have fallen from her pockets before she took off again. She forced her head to stay in the game and concentrate on the terrain because another injury would mean certain death, be it in the woods or a hospital. The moment Mina was on the grid again, The Madame would take her down.

Her head took that moment to pound once, just to drive the point home. She moaned and then shook away the fog. The Madame would not win this game of cat and mouse. The Madame might have more resources, but she relied on others to do her bidding— others who weren't hell-bent on protecting their own lives. Mina had more skin in the game than anyone on the other team.

As she walked, she forced herself to focus on the person in the truck. Her head throbbed with the effort it took, but she concentrated on the first time it drove through the neighborhood. It was the truck that stuck out. It was old and rusty but silent, which meant its power was being disguised. A truck that old and beat-up should have chugged like a mother down the street. That was her first clue something was off.

Her mind's eye zeroed in on the driver's side window on the second pass. A baseball cap. Just one. There was no one in the passenger seat. Mina cursed the fall sunset because it was already too dark to make out any features of the driver when he went

te cloud, but I still don't know if that's going
us."

e been assured that the data will only be used
nd if a sting needs to take place. Think of it
ding a blueprint for the case. Once we raid
use and arrest its leader, we can subpoena the
ation in the app. That's why we're sending you
pply. You can write the app while you're in-
e house learning the operation and ferreting
there are more girls involved."

ait," Roman said. "You want her to go in as
ployee and not as an escort?"

hey aren't looking for escorts, are they?" the
asked with his brow raised. "Those girls are
brought in from somewhere else. What they
right now is someone with skills who they can
ut, at the same time, tempt with the carrot of
ity."

hey need a girl with skills but one who is liv-
n the edge of society. Someone with no family,
pe and no ties to anything," Mina translated
noticed the SAC nod while she was reading.
y need a girl who is going to jump at a chance
his to have steady housing and three meals a
The problem is, most girls living that close to
dge don't have the training or skills to build an
How many have applied?"

rom what the Kansas office tells me, they've in-
ewed over a dozen but turned all of them away.
ve got three hours to read that file and learn

by at six o'clock. It was a man, though. He had to be a scout. The Madame would never send just one man to take Mina out. She wouldn't leave the job to chance. Her guys weren't trained agents looking to survive the next twelve hours. When your life was on the line, your motivation superseded anyone else's determination to finish a job.

Blazing white anger filled Mina. Anger at her bosses, who insisted she take the undercover position with The Madame, and anger at her partner for not having her back.

"Special Agent in Charge Moore, you wanted to see us?" Mina stood next to her partner, Special Agent Roman Jacobs, who was just as curious as she was to learn why they'd been summoned.

"Sit, please." He motioned at the two chairs in front of him. After they were settled, he leaned against his desk and crossed his ankles. It was a tell he didn't know he had, so Mina braced herself for what came next.

"I need an undercover agent."

Mina worked hard not to smile. Of course he did.

"You're going to need all of your expertise and experience for this one, Agent August."

"What's the job, SAC?"

He walked behind his desk and grabbed two files off the top, handing one to each of them. "Red Rye, Kansas. The word on the street is the house is a brothel."

"A brothel in the middle of Kansas?" Roman

asked, flipping open the file. "Prostitution is illegal there. Why wouldn't the city police deal with it?"

"Because from the outside, it's being billed as a legal escort service."

"Pay the girls for companionship and not sex," Mina translated.

The SAC snorted. "Sure, and the Vikings are going to win the Super Bowl this year."

Mina tried hard not to snicker. There was zero chance of that happening.

"We're in Minnesota," Roman said, pointing out the obvious. "Isn't there someone on the Kansas team who can take this?"

"No," SAC Moore said, sitting down behind his desk. "They're stretched thin and don't have any women who can go undercover inside the house."

"An undercover male could get the same job done," Mina suggested. "A simple john sting is all that's needed here."

The SAC shook his head and motioned at the folders, giving them time to read them. Mina scanned them, but her confusion grew with each page she turned.

"Why can't they find any of these girls in the database?"

"Excellent question," SAC Moore said. "And they think more girls are involved."

"You mean they think there are more houses with more girls?"

"Yes," he said with a nod. "Our Kansas office

thinks this may be a branch o[f]
Red Rye is in the middle of nov[here]
driving distance of five or six bi[g]
have images and videos of the [girls]
but our facial recognition syst[em isn't turn]
ing on them."

"They're ghosts," Roman sa[id]
"So to say. It's hard to be a ghost [...]
Whether they are ghosts by chan[ce...]
the other question."

Mina lifted a brow, her curios[ity...]
want me to ferret out if there are [...]
where these girls are coming from[...]

The SAC answered with a head [...]

"Why Mina, though?" Roman [...]
ner's protectiveness coming throug[h...]

"We need someone with her skills[...]
ing a printed sheet over the desk f[or...]
"They're advertising for a recepti[onist]
position. The ideal candidate has [...]
building skills."

Mina glanced at Roman and t[...]
"They want to build an app to hide [...]
tivities with legal ones."

"Most likely. And you have the s[...]
app and log everything that goes o[n...]

"Maybe. I'm not sure that eviden[ce...]
able in a court of law since it woul[d...]
tained illegally," she pointed out. [...]
to write in a backdoor that holds th[e...]

a priva[te...]
to help[...]

"I'v[e...]
when [...]
as bui[lding...]
the ho[use...]
inform[...]
in to [...]
side t[...]
out if[...]

"[...]
an er[...]

"[...]
SAC [...]
being[...]
need[...]
vet t[...]
stab[...]

"[...]
ing [...]
no h[...]
and [...]
"Th[...]
like [...]
day.[...]
the [...]
app[...]

"[...]
terv[...]
You[...]

your backstory. You've got skills, but no family or friends. Your drug addiction consumed the last few years of your life, but now that you're clean, you're looking for a better life. You've been scrubbed and recreated. Make this happen. The plane is waiting. You leave in thirty minutes."

"What's my role?" Roman asked, standing when Mina did.

"You're her partner," the SAC said, "regardless of where she is or who she is. You're her eyes and ears outside of that house in Red Rye. You'll be briefed if she gets the job. I want you to go with her today, and while she's interviewing, scout the address in the file as a possible home base. Report back when the interview is over, and we'll wait for them to call. New phones and IDs are on the plane. You have an hour in the air and two in the car to learn it."

"Thanks for the heads up," Mina muttered.

"I know there isn't much lead time, but I was given the same courtesy. Today is only the interview. When it's over, you'll have a couple of days to get your affairs in order here before you head back to Red Rye."

"You're rather confident, SAC," Roman said with a slight grin on his face.

"Well, let's just say my people will be in touch with their people, one way or the other. Mina, your disguise is on the plane. A wig today, and dye job tomorrow. You're going in as a blonde, confident,

*sexy computer coder who doesn't put up with bull
but is willing to help anyone who needs it."*

"That shouldn't be hard for her then," Roman
said, wearing a smirk, *"other than the blonde part."*

Anger swamped Mina as she pushed through the
woods. The guy who was supposed to have her back
turned out to be a dirty fink, too. The thought of
Roman Jacobs had her stomping across the muddy
ground until the sharp pain in her left foot reminded
her why she had to tread lightly in life now. She
would never be an undercover agent again because
of Roman Jacobs.

Her heart paused in her chest at the thought and
paused again when it added *right?* to the statement.
The memories she was positive were the truth a year
ago had slowly lost their authenticity. She realized
the dreams, the nightmares, were tangible memories of what happened that night. Those eyes she saw
dragging her to the window for fresh air haunted her.

Forcing her mind away from the dreams, she
slowed her steps. The pervading silence lulled her
into an easy rhythm until she heard something that
sent a shiver of fear skittering down her spine. Mina
froze in place and tipped her ear toward the road.
Tires on pavement. She hid the dim light, not that
she thought anyone could see it from the road, but
it wasn't worth taking the chance. She moved to a
large tree in silence and plastered herself behind it.
Waiting. Listening.

The vehicle was on the road to her left. Likely a

drunk coming home from the bar, but she'd stay put until it passed. No sense in tempting fate this early in the adventure. Not that anyone could see her in this forest full of foreboding trees, but she had an open field to cross soon, and she couldn't afford to make any mistakes.

She slid down the trunk of the tree and pulled her long raincoat under her butt before she sat. If she had to bed down right there for a few hours, she would, but in the meantime, she'd give her back a rest from the heavy pack. Mina rested her head against the trunk of the tree and closed her eyes. It had been a long day and a longer night. Once the coast was clear, she'd dig out some Advil and water before she soldiered on to her destination. She told herself the Advil was for her headache, but the aching pain that rumbled through her foot made a liar out of her.

Chapter Three

Roman slid into the grass before he shut the truck's door with barely a click. A glance around the area assured him the truck was hidden behind a long row of wrapped round hay bales. It wouldn't stay hidden come daylight, but hopefully, he'd be in it long before the sun came up. He would move forward on foot then double back for the truck once he had Mina with him.

Crouching alongside a hay bale, he asked himself what he was doing. *The right thing*, a voice reminded him. Mina was his. She had been for years, both as a partner and a friend. There was once a time when he thought they could be more. It was a senior agent who stressed that a workplace relationship was never a good idea. He was right, but she still dominated his every thought, even if those thoughts speared him with guilt. Living with the guilt that permeated every ounce of him was exhausting. He had to make things right and, hopefully, convince Mina they could still be partners.

His huffed breath shot a white plume into the air.

As if he stood half a chance of convincing Mina to come back to the FBI. He'd be lucky if she didn't shoot him and leave him for dead. Roman distractedly patted his ribs where his shoulder harness hung. He would never shoot Mina, but he was willing to shoot anyone out to hurt her.

Roman's plan to wait for her to emerge from the trees ended when he realized she could run through the woods for hours and never cross the road. He'd regrouped at a gas station just outside of Chester and used Google Maps to get a bird's-eye view of the area. Then he used his knowledge of Mina and his training as an agent to figure out her route. There were abandoned structures in the overhead view perfect for cover during the day. If he were Mina, that was what he'd do. Hide in the daytime and run at night. His only option was to intercept her at one of those buildings. The first one on the map was just up the road a few miles. He couldn't be sure which direction she would go, so he was taking a chance that she was using the woods to head toward a big city rather than push west into the remote forest.

He would choose the big city, and they'd been partners long enough for him to know she'd do the same. He darted across the road, thankful his boots were silent on the concrete. He cursed the rain for soaking him on his dash through the woods, but at the same time, he was grateful it covered the sound of his footfalls. Mina had a jump on him in terms of run time, but he had the advantage of a vehicle for the last two hours. He also had the benefit of two good feet. She didn't, so he'd taken that into account when he calculated the distance between her house and the abandoned structure. He checked his watch. It had been six hours since he'd found the footprints on the gravel road. It was nearing three in the morning, and he was tired, but he wasn't giving up on Mina August.

Running over soggy ground and jumping over mossy logs had his heart rate up when the wooden structure came into view. The front of it faced the river, which told him it was once someone's fishing cabin. It had seen better days. The windows were grimy, and the ones facing him had holes in several panes. The roof was missing logs, and the building listed a bit to the right. Regardless, it would still hide his partner well.

He paused next to a tree and waited, slowing his respirations and getting his head in the game. The rain was covering every sound now as it pounded down on the canopy of trees. Assessing the building wholly shrouded in darkness, Roman realized his mistake. There was no way to approach it without getting shot if she had a gun. If she didn't have a gun, she'd run. He racked his brain to come up with options that didn't involve him dying at her hands. She likely wouldn't hesitate, given what she believed about him.

It wasn't true.

He didn't desert her. Just the opposite was true.

Mina wouldn't be alive if he hadn't been there that night. She didn't remember that part, so he couldn't hold it against her. That self-hatred and guilt filled his gut and head, but he forced it away. There was time for that later. Roman knew he had to find a way to get her to trust him within seconds of their next encounter. He had to act right this minute before Mina took off again. A thought struck him, and Roman took a deep breath, praying Mina was inside the cabin. He clapped his hands together once, kicked a tree twice and clapped again, hopefully loudly enough for her to hear. He waited, but when he got no response, he repeated the pattern. It was the handshake they did every time they signed onto shift together. At least it was before she'd gone undercover.

Was that movement? He scanned the area around the cabin and caught the flash of a black shadow at the last second before it darted into the trees. Roman took off running without worrying about if she had a weapon. He wasn't going to let her get away. He refused to yell and let it be known they were out there to anyone else tracking them through these woods. His mission was to rescue her, not get them both killed.

With his legs pumping hard over the fallen logs, he was on her in a heartbeat. He grabbed her arm and spun her around but blocked her right jab simultaneously with his other arm. "Mina!" he hissed, his voice low and desperate. "I'm not going to hurt you! You don't need to run from me."

Her body was taut and ready to spring. Roman couldn't let his guard down. She would run again if he gave her a chance. That was Mina. Even if she knew she was going to lose, she was still going to try. "What are you doing here, Roman?" Her question was hissed more than it was asked.

The tree branches practically snatched her words into their trunks, and he had to lean in to hear her. "Trying to help you."

"Like you helped me a year ago? Thanks, but no thanks. I'll go it alone."

She tried to wrestle her arm out of his grip, but he held tightly to it. "There are two groups headhunting you, Min. I know you think you can go it alone, but if you want to survive the next forty-eight hours, you're going to have to trust me."

Roman finished his proclamation and stared into the eyes of the woman he hadn't seen in too long. She was gorgeous in a girl-next-door kind of way. Thank goodness she was no longer a blonde, and her golden-brown hair was partially tucked inside a stocking cap. He wanted to pull the hat off just to watch it fall free. That was always the favorite part of his day. The moment they'd finished a shift, and she'd pull that band out of her hair and let herself relax.

Tonight, all Roman wanted to do was regain her trust, and there was only one way to do that. Prove to her what went down that night in Red Rye wasn't his fault. That didn't mean seeing her again for the first time in a year wasn't messing with his head. It was, but he had to keep his eyes on the prize, and the prize was finally in his hands.

"The Madame and the FBI?" she asked, her tone so low he felt the vibration through her arm more than he heard the words. He nodded mutely but kept his gaze trained on hers.

He watched her fight with the two choices she had. Go it alone and face the bad guys down to certain death or trust him and stand a fighting chance of staying alive. He witnessed the moment she accepted her fate, and a tentative smile lifted his lips upward.

ROMAN JACOBS WAS the last person she expected to find her in these woods. He may have been her partner at one time, but if he thought she would trust him blindly for that reason alone, he was wrong. Mina's gaze traveled over him in quick assessment. He was still six kinds of yum sold as a variety pack. She wasn't tiny at five feet eleven inches, but Roman still intimidated her at his six feet three inches. He had enough bulk behind those inches that rarely did anyone resist his requests in the field. They'd had a few suspects try to push back, but they failed miserably against a guy like Roman.

He still tucked his jet-black hair behind his ears, and the curl at the ends gave him a boy-next-door look that softened his physique when he relaxed. The number of times she thought about running her fingers through that hair to see if the locks were as soft as they looked embarrassed her now. How moony she'd been over the guy when he was conspiring against her all along. At least that was what she kept telling herself so she didn't cry at the thought that he'd not only kept looking for her but found her.

His gaze raked her, and his sharp brown eyes were still as assessing and unnerving as they always were. He was a favorite with the ladies everywhere, but he never dated coworkers. That was his cardinal rule he insisted he would never break. She scoffed. His other cardinal rule he swore he'd never break was to always have his partner's back, but he'd epically blown that one last year.

"Let's use the cabin to get out of the rain, and we'll make a plan there."

"How did you get here?" Mina asked, taking a step back. She noticed his grimace but refused to give him the satisfaction of stepping forward again.

Instead of answering, he took her hand and tugged her back to the edge of the tree line. A look left, right and left again was all he did before he dashed for the dilapidated cabin that was supposed to be her salvation. Now she prayed it didn't end up being her grave. She tried to keep up with him, but her left foot didn't allow it. When she went down on one knee, he came up behind her, scooped her up and deposited her inside the cabin in what felt like one motion. He certainly hadn't lost any of his strength over the last year.

Mina snugged herself into a corner and waited while he closed the pathetic excuse for a door. It would keep them dry, but it wouldn't stop anyone who wanted in. Keeping her voice low, she asked the question burning in her mind. "How did you get here?"

"In a truck that I paid cash for in Minnesota. Plates are still registered in the other guy's name. The phone is off and untraceable."

"Where's the truck now?"

He stepped forward, his sweet, brown-eyed gaze eating up all the lines of pain and fatigue she couldn't hide on her face. "About a mile back in a farmer's field behind some hay bales. It's safe until we can get back to it."

"Wrong," Mina said immediately. "That truck is dead to us now. Who else knows you're here? Did you tell anyone your plans or ask for help?"

"No one," he promised, crossing his heart like a third-grader. "The FBI knows I've been looking for you since that night in Red Rye. I told SAC Moore I was burned out and taking a leave of absence. As far as he knows, I never found you."

She pushed off the wall of the cabin and refused to let the pain in her foot bring a grimace to her lips. "We gotta move." When they were shoulder to shoulder, Mina held up a finger. "Correction, I gotta move. You need to go home."

"That's not happening," he insisted. "People want

you dead, but I'm not one of them. You have to trust someone before it's too late, Min."

Anger spiraled low in her belly, and fire spit from her lips. "First, stop calling me Min. I'm not your buddy anymore. Second, trust you? Gosh, you mean like when I trusted you last year?" Her words were more of a snarl than a question. "Thanks, but no thanks, Jacobs. I hereby free you of any guilt or misguided duty you feel to save me from my enemies. They're my problem. Not yours."

"Wrong," he inserted before her last word died off. "They were our problem then, and they are our problem now."

"If they were our problem then, why did you abandon me?" she asked, the satisfaction of finally getting to ask that question tempered by the wave of pain flooding his eyes.

"I didn't abandon you. I never got the green light to go in! By the time I realized something was wrong, the place was already in flames."

She waved his words away. "It doesn't matter right now. This is my battle to fight. Go home while you still can. My life has been over since I first stepped foot in that house in Red Rye. I was a dead woman walking and didn't even know it. Now, I know it. You'd be better off walking away now with your life."

"We all thought The Madame snatched you until we figured out that she was still looking for you, too. How did you escape in that kind of condition?"

Roman asked, clearly ignoring her impassioned plea to leave.

Mina relaxed her face and prayed her eyes didn't hold the horrors of those early days on the run. The Madame had hobbled her before the fire and left her to die. While the doctors did their best, they couldn't put crushed bones back together in perfect alignment. It was like a jigsaw puzzle with pieces that were all the same color. The memories of the pain she suffered while trying to stay alive stole her breath away.

"I managed," was all she was able to say. Roman's raised brow told her he would never settle for that answer, but it was all she had time for right now. When he opened his mouth to speak, she jumped in. "Go home, Jacobs. I don't want you here."

He stepped up into her space and took hold of her raincoat, the material crinkling in his tight grip. His heat radiated through the material to warm her head to toe, and she remembered why she had a love-hate relationship with Roman Jacobs. He was either intensely possessive or flippantly aloof, and there was no in-between. Right now, his possessiveness of her was evident, if not a little bit surprising. He had always been hands-off with her, but he certainly wasn't following his cardinal rule tonight.

"Listen to me, Wilhelmina August, and listen good. Since the day I walked into your hospital room and found that bed empty, I've searched for you. Not out of guilt or a misguided sense of duty but because you are my friend and my partner. Partners don't let each other fight alone. Do you understand me?"

Her nod was her only answer. Mina's tongue was too tied staring into his coal-black eyes in the darkness of the little cabin to respond with words.

"Good. Now, let's get to my truck, and we'll find someplace safer than this." Roman released her coat and smoothed it down. "I need to get you somewhere safe and then secure the perimeter before we plan our next move."

Missing the heat of him up against her, Mina swallowed before she spoke so she didn't sound like a needy woman who hadn't been with a man in years. She hadn't been, but that was beside the point. She wouldn't give him the satisfaction of knowing how much it mattered that he was searching for her. Granted, she'd prefer if he weren't here mucking up her plans and putting himself in danger, but she was still touched that he wanted to find her.

"As for your truck, you know, the one you parked behind a hay bale?" Roman nodded mutely, but his assessing gaze had switched to one of urgency. She'd seen it in his eyes so many times on the job. It was always her who pulled him back from doing something stupid to blow the whole case. "I'm waiting for it to hit you that we can never go back to that truck. As soon as the farmer is up to milk the cows, he'll notice it and call the cops. Bet that didn't cross your mind, did it?"

Her triumphant gotcha moment died on her lips

when he stepped tight to her again. Anger radiated from his core, but his words were measured when he spoke. "No, because I planned for two scenarios. The first was not finding you here and moving on to the next abandoned shelter I found on the map. The second was finding you, dragging you back there immediately and getting you the hell out of here. What I failed to do was plan for the third scenario, which was typical Mina August obstinance."

Chest to chest, she stuck her finger in his. "I am not obstinate. I'm cunning, careful and precise. You worked with me long enough to know that I think before acting, unlike the person standing before me. You have no right to tell me how to conduct my life, Jacobs. I've been out here keeping my hide alive for a year without your help. Don't think I can't continue that trend now that you're here—"

A loud explosion cut off her words, and they plastered themselves up against the cabin wall. Roman held out a hand, signaling for her to remain in place while he worked his way around the perimeter to the back window of the cabin. A glance through the grunge-covered window revealed the glow of a fire in the distance. He hustled back to her and gave his head a shake.

"I do believe the truck option has been taken off the table."

Mina swallowed hard around the panic in her chest. "Why would someone blow up your truck? Were you followed?"

"I don't know that someone did, but the fire is in that direction, so regardless, a good number of emergency vehicles are about to descend on that location. What say we get out of here? We've got time to work our way out of range of that onslaught and find a new shelter for the daytime hours."

With a nod, she tightened the straps on her backpack and pulled the hood back up over her head. She forced herself to keep her mind clear of anything but the steps they needed to take to get to the next shelter. Her foot ached, and so did her head, but she'd push through it if it meant she could ride out of Bismarck with her life.

Chapter Four

Roman pulled up tight to the cabin door and waited for his partner to fall in behind him. They had an open area about twenty feet wide before they'd hit the tree line running. Well, an open area might be an overstatement. It was more like an area over-grown with weeds, but unfortunately, they weren't tall enough to use as cover.

He was sure of one thing—the fireball he'd seen in the sky was his truck. He was trying to protect Mina's tenuous trust in him and her thin grasp of sanity by being indirect about it. The Madame blew his truck up, which meant someone in their organiza-tion had him under surveillance, and he hadn't seen them coming. He was positive he didn't leave any electronic trails, nor was he followed out of Chester. Regardless, he was going to get her out of this alive if it killed him. He grimaced at the thought because engaging with The Madame could end in that result.

"After I give the all-clear signal, stay behind me and follow me directly into the woods."

"I can't run well," she hissed from behind him,

and he bit back a sigh before it escaped. That would only serve to make her mad—madder. Besides, the sigh wasn't in anger at her, but at himself for allowing The Madame a chance to hurt her.

"I know. We'll take it slow and easy, but we still can't be exposed for longer than necessary. Ready?"

She grabbed the back of his coat and leaned in over his shoulder. Even surrounded by the fetid scent of rotting vegetation, he could smell the sweetness of her apple-blossom shampoo. It took him back to when they used to smile and laugh together—a time before The Madame.

"What's the plan if we're ambushed?"

"We fight. That's the only move we've got. Do you have a gun?"

"Yes, but using it might alert others to our location."

"Good point. We avoid guns at all costs. I'm sure we have time to find cover, but we have to go now."

She tapped him on the shoulder in a fast one, two, three, and he knew it was time to take that step out the cabin's door. He inhaled and stepped out with Mina tight on his back. There was nothing he could do about the blind corners, but chances were good whatever entity had set the truck on fire hadn't made the mile run to the cabin yet. First, they'd have to know it existed.

Gauging the distance, Roman picked a speed he hoped Mina could keep up with on her damaged foot. She was in pain. He could see it on her face when she moved wrong, but there was little he could do about it until he could get them somewhere safe with a modicum of modern services. He had noticed the dried blood on her forehead and had to fight with himself not to check that injury, too. He didn't have time to worry about either right now. First, he had to get them to the tree line. His head on a swivel, he headed for the dark overhang of branches twenty feet away. He would have preferred they walk back-to-back, but he didn't suggest it. She could barely walk facing forward without falling.

They hadn't taken more than three steps when a shadow stepped away from the corner of the building. The man was dressed in black, silent and packed a hell of a punch. Roman was ready for it, and the quiet *oof* he made was overpowered by the cry of the assailant when Roman pulled his arm behind his back and snapped his wrist. A fast uppercut with his knee to the guy's chin had him dropping like a sack of potatoes to the ground.

A commotion behind him drew his attention, and he spun to see Mina trying to fight off a guy twice her size and doing a decent job of it. She had the guy in a headlock, but he was about to flip her to her back, and she didn't know it. Roman ran at him, ramming his head right into the guy's kidney and pushing him off his partner. They rolled together on the hard, cold ground in a tangle of arms and legs while Roman tried to gain the upper hand. Mina got it when Roman ducked, and she gave the guy a swift kick to the head with her tactical boot. He dropped over, a trickle of blood running from the split skin at his temple.

Roman jumped up, and they went back-to-back, turning in a circle while they waited for the next threat. When no one else joined in the fray, Mina asked the question he was thinking. "They only sent two?"

"Probably scouts. There'll be more on the way. We need to tie them up and ditch before they arrive."

"Grab his bootlaces." She pointed at the guy she'd just drop-kicked. "I'll get the one with the broken arm."

He heard the hint of laughter in her voice as she broke away from him and made quick work of getting the first guy's shoelaces free of his boots. Roman focused on her and nothing else. The way she moved with such precision always made him wonder what she'd feel like moving over and around him. He shook his head and ducked away, grabbing the leg of the unconscious man in front of him. He had to stop thinking about Mina as anything other than someone he had to protect. She was his mission and his responsibility. If he thought of her in any other way, he was going to get them both killed.

He quickly hog-tied the guy on the ground and was ready to grab Mina's hand to head out when the scout groaned and opened his eyes. Mina had fashioned a gag out of the other guy's hat, and Roman reached down to do the same when she grabbed his arm.

"Wait." She stood over the scout and grabbed his hair, lifting his head out of the dirt. "Who sent you?"

"You have no idea who you're messing with," he croaked rather than answer her question.

Roman bent down and yanked his tied hands tighter to his head, lifting his legs into even more of a pretzel. "The lady asked you a question. You'd do well to answer it."

"The Madame," he said, barely able to get the words out from the compression of his chest against the ground. "New wave coming. She'll never give up."

"Yeah, well, neither will I," Mina promised, then slammed the guy's head into the ground until he went slack. After she shoved the hat into his mouth, she stood up straight. "We need to go."

In one step, Roman grabbed her and swung her up into his strong arms. His long strides ate up the terrain, putting distance between them and the cabin that could have been their grave. He wouldn't let that happen again. From now on, he was the first line of defense whether the woman in his arms liked it or not.

MINA SLAPPED HER hand against Roman's hard chest. "Put me down!" Her words were barely a whisper in the silent forest, but he heard the anger in them loud and clear.

"A little further," he huffed, his steps not slowing even while carrying her one-hundred-and-thirty-pound frame, not to mention all her equipment. If she were honest with herself, being in his arms gave her a few moments of rest, but more than that, comfort. Comfort that had been missing in her life for more than a year. The comfort of home. The comfort of a hug from family. The comfort of a friend. The comfort of her partner in crime. As much as she hated to admit it, the few minutes of comfort this ride offered her, not only to her foot but to her soul, might give her the strength she'd need to push through this to the other side. She just couldn't let him know that, or he'd use it to his advantage.

Roman slowed as they neared the riverbank, the sky still dark even as it neared five o'clock. They would have to follow the riverbank a few hundred feet before they could dodge back into the trees and head toward Bismarck. When he lowered her to the ground, she noticed he took a step back. He was probably waiting for a punch or a tongue lashing. He wouldn't get either.

"Thank you," she whispered, her breath puffing white into the air as the early morning temps hovered in the forties. "For the ride and for saving my butt back there. I'd be dead if you hadn't shown up when you did." A shiver ran through her. She didn't know if it was the cold wind or the idea of death at the hands of The Madame. Worse yet, being a hostage.

Roman rubbed her arms up and down, probably thinking the shiver was from the cold. "Maybe, maybe not. I've learned you never count Wilhelmina

August out of any situation. Besides, I might be the one who led them straight to you. I swear no one followed me, and I told no one where I was going."

"They didn't need to follow you. All The Madame had to do was put a tracker on you somewhere. It was common knowledge that you were my partner. They could follow you anywhere without showing their faces."

Roman ran a hand through his thick, black hair and sighed. "I checked everything religiously and never found a tracker."

"What are you wearing from Minneapolis? Anything they could have a tracker in without your knowledge?"

"No, my clothes and boots I bought right off the shelf at the farm store. There's no way there's anything in them. My watch, wallet and phone were in the truck."

"Did you use your phone tonight?"

"I searched Google Maps, but the phone is a burner."

"Did you leave the truck unattended at any point?"

Mina didn't need confirmation. She could see it on his face before he answered.

"I had to a few times to sleep, eat and shower. Once again, I dropped the ball. I didn't think anyone was following me or would know the truck was mine."

Mina punched him gently on the shoulder. "Don't beat yourself up too much, partner. They were going to find me one way or the other. All you did was accelerate the timeline. I should probably thank you for that because moving every three months was a real pain in my backside." She laughed, but he didn't join her.

"I dropped the ball, Mina, again. I'm sorry."

She shrugged and straightened the pack on her back. "We can't go back in time, but we can move forward. That's our only move now. Look at it this way, Roman. If I'm going to survive a resurgence of The Madame and walk out alive again, I'm going to need all the help I can get."

"Why else would I be here?" Roman asked, his shoulders straightening now that he had his breath back.

"To kill me." Mina noticed the three words hit him like bullets. "But since you just saved my bacon back there, I don't think that's why you're here."

"The very last thing I want is to kill you. Lock you up in a room to keep you safe from The Madame is what I want to do. I know that isn't going to happen, though, so I'm following your lead. Where are we headed?"

"North."

"That's what they'll expect, though. Following the river is a dangerous ploy."

"We don't have a choice," she insisted, her breath tight in her chest. "We need to get to Bismarck, where my storage unit is with a car and a new life. Going south only leads us back to them."

"We need to get back to Minneapolis, Mina. There are people there who will help you."

"No," she hummed, sticking her finger in his chest. "I won't set foot back in that city until we know where The Madame is and why no one came to help me that night. Trust no one. I shouldn't even trust you!"

Roman wrapped his hand around her finger and held it patiently. "I hear what you're saying. I understand your reasoning, but you have nothing to fear from me. I want you to be free to live your life without looking over your shoulder. That's the only reason I'm here. If you want to go north, we'll go north."

The air stolen from her sails, Mina hesitated. He was right. The Madame knew their last location, and she'd expect them to go north. If they made it to Bismarck—and that was a big if with The Madame this close—it would take them days. Days her pursuers wouldn't need with a vehicle at their disposal.

"There's no way to beat them to Bismarck now that they know where we are. We probably have ten, maybe twelve hours tops, to get to Bismarck and get back out before they catch up to us again. It's over twelve hours of walking from here."

"And that foot of yours isn't going to last twelve more hours. It's almost daylight, and we are out of options except one. Do you want to hear it?"

"Do I have a choice at this point?"

"Not that I can see," Roman said with a grin, "but I'll wait while you decide for yourself."

She punched him again, harder this time to remind him she could hold her own. "Fine, hit me with it."

"We go east. It's all farmland. Where there are farms, there are…"

"Farm trucks," she filled in, and he nodded once. "Stealing a truck will be tricky. Once we have it, we're still in danger driving down the highway."

"All of that is true, but we only have two choices. We get a truck and drive or start walking and risk running into more of The Madame's merry men."

"If we can get a truck, we could be at the storage unit in a couple of hours. If we get that far, we're home free. The car will get us to a hotel where we can rest and make a new plan."

He pulled a piece of paper from his pocket and held it out, shining his penlight on the map. "I marked all the areas with civilization before I came out. I know this is a farm," he said, pointing at a crudely drawn roof.

"We have to cross the road to get to it, though." Mina ran her finger along the two-lane highway that cut through the patch of trees they were hiding in.

"We're out of time, Min. Just remember, when we get there, we have a vehicle, and you can give your foot a rest. Focus on that."

Her nod was one and done, then she turned to the east and glanced behind her. "Ready?"

"Lead on. I'll follow you anywhere, Agent August."

Mina took off through the trees as fast as she could, and Roman matched his steps to hers. As the wet branches whipped her face and soaked her clothing, all she could think was Roman Jacobs was either her savior or her downfall. She knew him, and she knew his skills. He had been a top-notch agent his entire career until he failed to provide necessary backup to his partner, nearly leading to her death. Before that event, he was the kind of guy she would trust with her life. Mina's gut said that was still true, but she didn't have time to hash out the particulars of that night with him right now. First, they had to dodge the people hunting them. She was out of options, so if Roman Jacobs was the enemy, it was wise to keep him close.

Chapter Five

Something had finally gone her way in this mess. They'd made the trek to the farm in record time, motivated by the idea of a chance to dry out on the ride to Bismarck. Their first bit of good luck came when they found an old farm truck parked behind a barn. It was more rust than metal, but it had plates and was used recently if the hay in the bed was any indication.

Mina flipped the visor down, and the keys fell into her lap with a jingle. She shook them at Roman, who grinned and started pushing the truck through the grass to the old road. Thankfully, it was far enough away from the farmhouse that they wouldn't have to use the driveway and alert the farmer. She wouldn't start the truck until they were ready to pull onto the highway, just to be sure they weren't heard. The rain was working in their favor, too. While they were wet and cold, the cloud cover kept the stars and moon at bay and gave them more time to escape unseen before daybreak. With any luck, they'd be at her storage unit before the sun came up.

After glancing up and down the highway for

lights, Roman motioned for her to start it up. He jumped in, and she headed north up the highway, the heater on high to blast out enough warm air to dry them. Mina wanted to close her eyes, but she refused to let Roman drive. He didn't know where the storage unit was, which simple directions could have fixed, but she didn't trust him. He would take her back to Minneapolis, where everyone was a foe, and no one was a friend.

"If you need a break, just say the word. I'm not going to turn the truck around and head back to headquarters. You can trust me."

Her chuckle released some tension in her chest. "You always could read me like a book."

He smirked, and she forced her eyes to stay on the road. If they didn't, she'd probably crash the truck when she got lost in his giant brown ones.

"That's why we worked so well together." He leaned his bulky frame against the door and his head on the window. "We didn't need words to know what the other was thinking, and that saved us a lot of time and saved a lot of lives."

"Until the one time it didn't," she muttered.

Roman didn't say anything. There was probably nothing he could say. He screwed up, and he knew it. Her eyes flicked to all the mirrors, but there were no headlights behind or in front of them. She kept a tight grip on the wheel as they plowed forward into the darkness. She was laser-focused on getting them to Bismarck, dropping the truck somewhere for the cops to find and then hitting the road again. She wasn't happy that she'd have to take Roman with her, but there was no doubt it was better to have him with her than out there leading the monsters to her door. If she knew one thing about him, it was his determination. He would never give up on her, so ditching him now would be useless. He was going to keep coming back until she let him help her. The problem was his determination could get him killed this time.

The clock said they'd been on the road for almost an hour. When Mina glanced over at him, his eyes were closed. His hair was still plastered to his head on one side from the rain, and he was still the most handsome man she'd seen since this madness began. Mina thought she was over her crush on Roman Jacobs after he nearly got her killed, but it turned out it was an out-of-sight, out-of-mind situation. Now that he was in sight, the crush was back full force.

Her sigh was heavy when it filled the cab of the truck. She should hate him with everything inside her for abandoning her that night. He said he never got the green light to go in. She turned that over in her mind a couple of times. She'd sent the SOS message, so why didn't he get it? Mina was confident in her coding skills, and the possibility that he didn't get the message shook her to the bone. If that were true, then that changed everything she believed over the last year. Regardless of the reason, he wasn't there for her that night.

He's here now.

This time the breath she blew out sounded like she'd been gut-punched. He *was* here now. He had taken a leave of absence to find his partner because that was Roman's code of honor. No man left behind. That was his motto in the army and as a civilian. He was insistent she would do the same thing if the roles were reversed. He wasn't wrong, but the difference was if the roles had been reversed, she would have done her job the first time to ensure he didn't have to run.

But if what he said was true, and he never got the SOS, that meant the message got hung up in the app, and it wasn't his fault. Her brain kept asking *what if*, but her heart kept refusing to answer. Her heart wanted to believe him with everything it had. If he was telling the truth and never got her message, then what happened that night was her fault. Then again, maybe someone intercepted it. It had crossed her mind that someone in The Madame's organization may have interfered with the message, but she was always so confident in her work that she refused to believe it. In the end, maybe it was her ego that caused the carnage that night.

"Are we there yet?" Roman asked into the quiet cab.

Mina jumped, torn from her musings by the man himself. "Almost," she answered after she cleared her throat. "Keep your eyes out for a place to dump the truck. I want the cops to find it and return it to the farmer."

"You kept your gloves on the whole time?" he asked, motioning at her hands with his chin.

"I'm not new at this, Agent Jacobs."

His strangled snort brought a smile to her lips. "Just checking. The storage unit you have, is it well lit?"

This time it was her sarcastic snort that brought a smile to his lips. "Define *well lit*. There are seven rows of units, and the only lights are at the front. I'm in row seven, which is in the far back and butts up to a field."

"On purpose." She lifted a brow but said nothing else. He wasn't asking a question. "Let's drive the truck to the unit then. We'll need the headlights to flush out anyone who might be waiting. Once it's clear, we'll move the truck to the front and leave it there. Someone will report it."

"That leads them directly to me, though." Mina shook her head. Did he think she was going to do that?

"Not at all. It leads The Madame directly to the storage unit, which knowing you, and I do, is sitting in the middle of nowhere. We won't be anywhere near it when the truck is found, likely a day or two from now. You used a fake name when you rented it, I assume."

"Of course," she agreed with a shoulder shrug.

"We need to protect your foot, Min. If we walk even a mile from where we leave the truck, that's a mile less your foot can do down the road if the need arises."

She refused to acknowledge his words or her weakness. "The Fairlane is packed and ready. Once I swap out Tactical Barbie for Hippie Barbie, we can get on the road."

He was grinning at her like a fool when she glanced at him from the corner of her eye. "Tactical Barbie. I love it. In my opinion, you are the furthest thing from a Barbie a man could find."

The truck was silent for two beats before she opened her mouth. "Did you just imply that I am nowhere near as attractive as Barbie?"

"No," he said instantly, his hands waving in the air. "Not what I meant at all. I just meant that I'm not into unrealistic body images for women. I hate it when people feed me a fake persona. That's all I meant."

"You're saying that, in a Roman Jacobs kind of way, that was a compliment."

"To the highest degree," he agreed. He must have noticed the lights of the town because he leaned forward and swiveled his head around the truck's perimeter. "How far out are we?"

"A few miles. I haven't seen another car the entire trip. Thanks for being the lookout, by the way." She had to rib him a little bit for sleeping on the job.

"I knew you'd wake me if we ran into trouble. I'll need to drive the next leg, so I decided to grab a few hours. Your turn is coming."

"Like hell," she muttered, slowing for the reduced speed limit sign. She went on high alert when the storage unit came into sight, and she braked as they drove past the driveway. She turned around, drove back and pulled into the gravel drive.

"We'll see about that," he shot back, leaning forward in his seat. "It looks empty. Drive through the rows like a figure eight. We need to make sure no one is waiting to ambush us."

She did as he instructed since she planned to do that anyway, but she bristled slightly. "There's no way The Madame knows about this place."

"I didn't think she was tracking me, either."

The truck fell silent as she concentrated on weaving in and out of the aisles of units until she got to the final row. No one was around, and the place was eerie in the early morning fog. "Let's do this as quickly as possible. I'm going to ditch the truck and work my way back. Give me five minutes. Have the car running."

Mina bailed from the truck, and he waited while she unlocked the unit and flashed her light inside for half a second. All was silent, and she gave him a thumbs-up before she pulled the door down. She knew their reprieve wouldn't last long.

Roman eyed the area around the convenience store, looking for places where The Madame could hide in wait for them. "What's the plan?" he asked the exhausted woman next to him.

Gone was the beautiful brunette he'd known for seven years. She'd been replaced by a beautiful red-head who would have fit right in sitting on the back of an old VW bus on her way to Woodstock.

"I have to use the restroom."

"Same. You go in first. When I know you're locked inside, I'll use the other one. Do not come out until I knock on the door and call to you. After our potty break, we have to decide where we're going."

Mina gave him a nod that said more than words could, and they both bailed out of the car. Roman leaned against the hood of the old Fairlane and watched the woman he'd gone through hell with a thousand times over walk into the restroom. *Walk* was a strong word. *Hobble* was more accurate. A grimace tugged at her gorgeous face with every step until she locked the door and blocked him out. She needed rest and time to heal. There was no question that life on the run the last year had prevented her foot from healing. Hell, knowing Mina, she probably hadn't seen a doctor since the day she left the hospital. He shook his head at her stubbornness and spun around on the hood, his gaze traveling around the area, assessing for threats from any blind corner. He was sure they had bought enough time that there wouldn't be any yet.

The Madame might have teams out looking for them, but they were still searching in the middle of North Dakota. Since they left the storage unit four hours ago, they'd logged enough miles to put them near the border of Minnesota. He suspected she didn't have a plan. She was simply driving in hopes of outrunning the bad guys. She was exhausted, in pain and not thinking clearly, but she wouldn't go down without a fight.

Roman spied a relic hanging on the side of the old building and jogged over to the pay phone, snapping on a glove before picking up the receiver. He was shocked to hear a dial tone on the other end. He hung it up, jogged to the restroom and took care of business, then knocked on her door. "Ready."

The lock clicked, and she stepped out, her face wet as though she'd washed it, but her eyes told him the real story. The water was to hide the tears of pain that had built up until they demanded release. Roman grasped her elbow, and she leaned heavily on him on the way back to the car. He lowered her to the passenger seat then knelt and rested his hand on her knee.

"You're tired. You need to let me drive, Min. I know you don't trust me, but I trust you, okay? I'll do whatever you tell me to, but I can't let you keep driving in the shape you're in right now."

Her nod was frustrated but agreeable. "I don't have a choice, I know. I'm running on fumes, and the pain has my mind muddled. All I know is once I find someplace safe again, you're going to take this Fairlane and get as far away from me as possible."

"Wrong," Roman said instantly, taking hold of her chin to force eye contact. "We're in this together, no matter what. Listen to me, I have a plan, but we both need to agree on it."

"Then you're a step ahead of me already. What's your plan?"

"I have an army buddy just outside of Fargo on the Minnesota side who we can trust. He has an encampment there that would let us safely disappear for a little while until we can figure out what The Madame wants."

"She wants me, Roman. She wants me." She jabbed herself in the chest with her finger on a grimace. "She thinks I know her secrets, and she won't quit until I'm dead."

He squeezed her knee gently until she quieted. "That may be, but they're only secrets until we tell the world. Your information in the hands of the right people will bring her down."

"You don't seem to understand that I can't trust anyone, Roman. Most especially you!"

"Shh," he whispered, glancing around. "I understand how you feel about that, but just hear me out. The only way we're going to function is to get some sleep. The only way to do that is to be protected. My friend can provide that."

"Your friend with the encampment," she repeated, and he nodded. "Is he a cop?"

Roman's laughter was quiet, but he was sure she could hear the amusement in it. "Not even a little bit. He's private security and…other things."

"Other things that are less legal?"

"He does a lot on the other side of the law, but he does them for the right reasons. That's all I can say."

"How do you know we can trust him? The Madame may have already found him as a contact of yours. He could be compromised."

"Cal is ex–military police."

"So are you," she pointed out on a lifted brow.

"Yes, but I went civilian mainstream, Cal… didn't. If The Madame sent anyone to his camp unannounced, they're already staring at six feet of soil. The things he does on the outside of the law are always for the good guys."

"He's a mercenary."

"He was, but with a code of honor toward his country and his friends. Now he runs a security business with our ex-military brothers." Roman pointed at the pay phone on the wall of the store. "I can call him and let him know we're coming. In less than two hours, you could be in a bed, asleep and protected for the first time in a year."

"Two years," she muttered, her eyes heavy.

"You've been MIA for a year, Mina."

"And undercover with The Madame for the year before that. Do you think I slept with both eyes closed there? Not for a hot second."

"I'd expect nothing less," he admitted with a chuckle "So, what do you say, partner? Should I call him?"

"No. We'll call him. We're putting him on speaker, and if you play any games, I'll use the Smith & Wesson under my belt to put you out of commission long enough for me to leave your sorry, unreliable butt in the dust."

Roman put his hands up and laughed. "I can accept those terms. The pay phone doesn't have a speaker, though. We'll have to snuggle up, and both listen in."

"I have burner phones. Get in and drive in that direction for thirty minutes. Let's make sure we didn't pick up a tail. If we're in the clear after that, we'll find a place to pull over and call your friend."

"I can work with that."

Before she could say more, he lifted her legs inside the car and closed the door then climbed into the driver's side. Once they were buckled in, he started the car and backed out of the spot, pulling onto the two-lane highway. He'd let her call the shots if he got what he wanted out of the deal, and what he wanted was a chance to put The Madame behind bars.

To do that, he had to prove to the woman next to him that he didn't abandon her when she needed him most. He had to prove the mission was compromised long before she tried to send that message. The guilt that filled his chest every time he looked at her had to go. It was killing him slowly from the inside out. The only way to do that was to find The Madame and prove his innocence.

Chapter Six

Mina had been more than a little bit surprised when Roman pulled into his friend's encampment. To her, that word conjured an image of tents and huts spread across an open field of overgrown grass. Instead, they were met at the gate by a guy who could easily have played linebacker for the Minnesota Vikings. He motioned them through the gate onto a sprawling estate with a grand lodge at the end of the long drive. Scattered behind the lodge were smaller log cabins that looked unassuming. Roman had assured her they were hiding bulletproof glass and walls as well as top-of-the-line communications and electronics.

Before Roman could put the car into Park, the door to the lodge opened, and a man stepped out. He was as big or bigger than Roman and close in age to Roman's thirty-five years. He was handsome, but his face showed the hard lines of a life lived doing bad things to help good people. Roman hopped out of the car and grabbed the man in a bear hug. Mina didn't need words to know their relationship went deeper than friends.

Her door swung open, and Roman helped her out of the car, keeping an arm around her waist while he introduced her. "Cal, this is my partner, Mina."

Cal stepped forward and shook her hand, a smile on his face. "Ah, yes, the infamous Wilhelmina August. I've heard many stories about you over the years. I'm more than a little bit relieved that Roman found you. He's been beside himself this past year." He motioned at the lodge behind him. "Welcome to Secure One. Come on inside so you can take that ridiculous wig off and get off your feet. From what I know of your case, you've been going it alone for a long time."

Mina's smile was tentative but accepting. "It's been a long fourteen months. I can't argue with you there."

Roman kept his arm around her waist and helped her up the few stairs to the lodge. She liked having his support too much for her own good, but she'd take it until she got some sleep and had a chance to reevaluate her options. She didn't have many, and without Roman and now Cal, she'd probably be dead. She tried to focus on the men in the woods who had jumped them. She wanted her mind to tell her that she recognized them from Red Rye. If she could link them to Red Rye, she could search the log of men she'd saved in the app's database. Her mind told her it had been too dark, and the adrenaline had been pumping too fast. Simply too tired to make sense of much, she stuck it on the back burner until she was rested.

"I've made up the guest suite for you," Cal said as he led them down a long corridor that sported a beautifully stained hardwood floor and shiplap on the walls. Her trained eye caught the thumb reader keypads by each room and the lights running along the baseboards for illumination in the dark. There was probably an integrated alarm and fire system throughout the entire lodge as well.

"A cabin would be fine," Roman said, smiling at her as he helped her along the hallway. It was barely wide enough for two people Mina's size, so having Roman next to her meant she was smashed up against him, her arm around his waist just to keep from tripping and falling. She could make it by herself, but he didn't seem to want to let go of her. While she liked her independence, being close to someone again hit her in a place she forgot existed. She didn't think it was her heart, either. It was something more profound than that. It was a connection with another soul that she hadn't had in too many years. It made sense she'd feel that way with Roman since he'd been such a pivotal part of her life for so long, but she was supposed to be mad at him for ditching her when she needed him most. She couldn't find the energy to worry about it tonight. Not when he tugged her back into him every time she tried to pull away. Not when she could still hear the words of the guy they'd taken out in the woods when he warned of a second wave. Roman had found them a place to stay, at least for tonight, and for that she couldn't be too mad.

"I'd rather you were buttoned up tight here," Cal said, stopping at the door with his thumb on the keypad. "I don't take chances with family."

"Family?" Mina asked as Cal pushed open the door. To the casual eye, the room behind it was a studio apartment with a small kitchen, two queen beds and a bath. To the trained eye, it was so much more. The hatch in the floor surrounded by a metal cage told her that much without her even stepping inside.

"What? Roman didn't tell you that we grew up together?" He punched Roman in the arm. "I'm hurt, man. Crushed."

Laughter spilled from Mina, and it surprised her. She hadn't laughed with true abandon since the last time she'd had Roman in her life. Even working undercover, he could make her laugh. A silly text or a clandestine meeting under the stars would have her giggling at his goofiness within minutes. She hadn't realized how much she missed laughing until that moment.

"I had no idea," she admitted. "Roman told everyone his family was dead."

"They are," Roman clarified, helping her into the room. "My parents died when I was two. I grew up in foster care until Cal's family took me in when I was five. Cal is my younger brother by three years."

"It's just me and Roman left now," Cal added.

"And Cal is a ghost, so I don't talk about him to other people," Roman explained. "That leads to entanglements that would put both Cal and me in a tight spot."

"I know he loves me, in his own big, bad agent kind of way. But he's right. I prefer to be off the radar if you know what I'm saying." He eyed Mina with a raised brow, and she nodded once in understanding.

"Now that we understand each other, welcome home. Everything you'll need is waiting, including meds for that foot. I doubt they'll fix much, but they might give you a few hours of sleep if nothing else. After you've rested, I'll show you the bunker. From what Roman tells me, you're a bit of an expert at being a ghost yourself. I have some equipment down there that'll help you with your pursuit."

"I'm ready now," she said eagerly. If Cal had a way to end this manhunt The Madame had put in motion, she was ready and willing to participate.

"No, you're not," Roman said, his tone firm. "You need a shower, food and sleep before you even think about going to the bunker. I know you, and once you get down there, you won't resurface until you've found and mitigated the threat."

Okay, so he wasn't wrong. Mina didn't have to like it, though. The fact was she'd already pushed her body past its breaking point six hours ago. Now, she was running on pure pain and adrenaline. The pain would last, but the adrenaline wouldn't.

Mina crossed her arms over her chest and huffed.

"I can't believe you talked me into this. I'm not supposed to trust anyone, and here I am, falling in line behind you two."

Roman stepped in front of her and grasped her shoulders. The way his gaze held hers made her wish she were alone with Roman the man, not Roman the federal agent. "Listen to me, Min. You are not falling in line behind us. You are always in the lead, and as I did for all the years before this, I'll follow you anywhere. We're here because I knew Cal had what you needed to find The Madame and take her down. We're the muscle to make sure you can put this woman behind bars and that you're alive when it happens. Do you understand what I'm saying?"

She nodded, but a memory flickered across her mind's eye, and she tried to grab it. There were those eyes again in that blazing inferno that looked a lot like the pair she was seeing now. Mina shook her head to clear it.

"Shower, food and rest. Then we attack."

"Good," Roman agreed with a nod before he turned back to Cal. "Looks like I owe you another round."

Cal walked to the door with a shake of his head. "Brother, you know your debts have long been paid in full. Family takes care of family. Shower, rest and share a meal with a friend you haven't seen in too long. Then we'll work. This door locks automatically from the inside. Once I leave, no one is getting in. If they try to smoke you out, you know how to get to the bunker." Roman nodded as he pulled Mina into him again in a sign of protectiveness. It was an action even she couldn't ignore.

Cal slipped out the door, and Mina turned to take in the room. "This is quite the place."

Roman's laughter was everything to her in that moment of uncertainty. When they worked together, that sound always grounded her in the certainty that they had each other's backs. She thought that had been lost to her forever, but now, she wasn't so sure.

"Cal doesn't do anything halfway. This space has all the comforts of home with the added benefit that it's impenetrable. His room is just like this one, but on the other end of the house. The rest of Secure One is staff rooms and a large dining room and kitchen for those staying in the cabins."

Roman pulled her wig off, removed the net holding her natural hair and used his giant paws to smooth it down the way it should be. His smile was tender when he hit her with it. "There's the woman I've been thinking about for a year. I'm so glad you're safe."

Before she could respond, he had her wrapped in his arms, her cheek against his warm chest, and his cheek resting on her head. She leaned into him, his heat a balm to her tired and sore body, but also her tired heart. A friend to help her was what she needed.

"I hope this is okay," he said, tightening his arms a bit before loosening them again. "I know we're partners, but I've wanted to hug you since that day in the hospital when you disappeared like smoke. I just wanted to hug you and tell you how sorry I was for not being there."

Her arms tightened around him, and she kept her head on his chest. "This is okay," she whispered. It took effort, but she held at bay the tears that wanted to fall at his admission. "I needed a friend. I'm happy you were the one to find me."

"You don't know how glad I am that I found you before those guys in the woods." She felt the shiver travel through him, but before she could speak, he did. "Listen, you're barely upright. How about a shower while I make you something to eat? Then, you get off that foot and sleep for the night. Tomorrow is soon enough to start the hunt."

While that sounded like heaven, Mina had to decide if she could sleep in the same room as Roman. The idea that he was here for any other reason than to help her finish off The Madame was becoming harder and harder to swallow. His actions weren't those of a man out to finish a job. His actions were of a man who was torn apart by guilt. He might be looking to finish a job, but that job wasn't to kill her. From what she could see, the job was to help her get her life back. Her old life, that was gone, but if she could still draw breath when The Madame was put behind bars, maybe she could cobble together a new life from the ashes of her old.

"Mina," Roman caught her arm before she turned away. "I know you must be angry. The one time you needed me, I wasn't there. We're partners, and I made promises I didn't keep."

Mina's sigh bore the weight of that night, and she noticed his lips blanch when he pulled them taut.

"What do you want me to say, Roman? Do you think if I admit that I'm angry about what happened in Red Rye that you'll somehow feel better? That your guilt will be appeased because I'm mad at you? After seven years, I thought you knew me better than that. Did things go sideways in Red Rye? Yes. Was it your fault? Should you shoulder the blame? No, not all of it. I went into the house knowing what the risks were and accepted them as the price of admission. I must bear the guilt and the blame for some of it as much as you. I don't know what happened, but I chose to go into that assignment knowing the risks."

"I should have known something was wrong, Min."

"Maybe, but here's the thing, Roman. Me being angry at you isn't going to make you feel better. You want to believe it will. You want me to scream at you for all your shortcomings so that you can turn that guilt in your gut back on me. I don't know what happened that night. I don't know who I can trust and who I can't trust. All I know is when you showed up in the woods last night, and you didn't take me out immediately, I had my answer. If you were working for The Madame, I'd be dead. At the very least, we'd be on our way to see her."

Roman stood mutely with his jaw pulsing while

his hands clenched and unclenched. He was never good at faking emotions. Her partner was always a "what you see is what you get" kind of guy. What she saw tonight wasn't anger but rather self-hatred. He hated himself for what happened that night, and while it made her sad that he had to live with that, it buoyed her at the same time. If he was this upset about what happened in Red Rye, then the chances she could trust him just went up.

"I would never hurt you on purpose, Min. I promised to have your back, and I let you down that night, but I have searched for you every day since. I had to find you and prove that I don't break all my promises."

"Life is what happens between the promises, Roman. You know that. Somewhere down deep, you know my decisions were going to affect your promises. That doesn't make it wrong. It just makes it what it is."

"What is it then?" Roman asked, his words filled with desperation even she didn't understand. "If it's not wrong, what is it? And don't say it is what it is."

"But it is," she said, her lips wearing a sad smile. "We can let it ruin who we are and drive a rift between us we can never bridge, or we can forgive ourselves for whatever we think we did wrong. Listen, it's like this, Roman. I'm thirty-five years old, and I've seen humanity at its worst. Together we've captured some of the most disgusting filth on the planet and put them away for good. I could ignore our past and what we did for six years together. We could both stomp off to separate corners and pout, but in the end, we're too old and in too much danger for childish behavior and miscommunication to be the reason we don't find The Madame. Do you agree?"

"I wouldn't be here if I didn't, Min. You had to know that I never gave up on you. You were my every thought. That's why I'm here."

"No man left behind," Mina said, but his head shook slightly.

"No. It had nothing to do with honor toward a partner or the job. Finding you had everything to do with worrying that my friend wasn't safe and that she needed me."

"I don't know a lot right now, Roman. I don't know who The Madame is. I don't know how I'm going to find her. I don't know if I'll be alive this time tomorrow, but I do know this. I can trust you." He grimaced, and she rested her hand over his. "You showed up. You put in the effort. You showed me that I was still important to you. So, while I don't know much, I do know that I've lived without you for a year, and it was the most miserable year of my life. I'm going to trust my instincts because they're all I've got. My instincts tell me I have nothing to fear from you."

Mina turned, and this time, her partner let her go.

Chapter Seven

A bloodcurdling scream had Roman on his feet with a gun in his hand before he opened his eyes. The next sound that registered was one he'd heard before from a scared child. Whimpering. This time, the sound came from his partner, and it almost destroyed him. He set the gun back on the table and walked to her bed, lowering himself to the edge, where he whispered to her.

"Mina, honey, wake up."

She was sweaty, and the bedcovers were twisted around her. She must have been thrashing in her sleep. Roman jogged to the bathroom and wet a washcloth under cool water, then returned to her bed. Mina's eyes were open, but her stare was blank. He wasn't sure anyone was home.

"Hey." He muttered the word at a level barely above a whisper so he didn't scare her. "That sounded like a bad dream."

Her chin trembled once before she swallowed. "I have them sometimes."

Those four words were enough to flare that ugly

fire of guilt in his chest. He smoothed the cloth across her overheated cheeks and straightened it to rest on her forehead. A shiver ran through her, and if that scream indicated the level of terror she experienced that night, it helped him understand how much pain she must have gone through. He rubbed her shoulder until the shivering stopped and her chest rose and fell once.

"Can I get you anything?" he asked, feeling useless to ease the pain and turmoil he most likely caused.

"Water," she said, her voice scratchy.

Roman jumped up and practically ran to the fridge for a cold bottle. While he was there, he grabbed more of the pain medication that Cal had left at his request. He cracked open the water bottle and returned to the bed to help her sit up. She leaned against the headboard and brought the bottle to her lips, a slight tremble in the motion until half the bottle was gone. He handed her the pills, and she swallowed those before he took the bottle from her and set it on the nightstand.

"Okay now?"

She nodded once before she tried to push the hair out of her face with trembling hands. Roman couldn't resist the urge to do it for her. He tucked her wavy locks behind her ears and offered a smile of understanding and solidarity. "It's only one a.m. I think we should try to get some more sleep. Cal will be up early, but not this early."

Mina held his hand in a death grip. "Don't go."

Roman covered her hand with his other paw and held tight. "You're okay. You're safe here."

"At least for tonight."

"No, forever. I'm not going to let The Madame take you away from me again. Okay? Try to relax."

The sway of her curls around her shoulders when she shook her head made his gut tighten. She was all beauty and grace even when she was tough as nails. She never let down her guard, so to see her this vulnerable and afraid made Roman realize how much she'd been through over the past year.

"I can't relax after that dream."

Another tremble went through her, and in one motion, he scooped her up and rested her on his lap. He wanted to moan his happiness to have her in his arms, but he bit it back. He didn't have that right. He didn't even have the right to hold her, but she needed comfort, and he was the only one here to offer it.

"What do you need, Mina?" he asked, resting his cheek on her head and inhaling the scent of French vanilla. Cal had gone all out when he stocked the room for them. Not only had he filled the bathroom with essentials, but he'd had a new wardrobe waiting for them both, a walking cane for her that Roman knew she'd never use and medication to help relieve some of the pain in her foot.

"I need to find The Madame." Her answer had him pulling himself back to the present.

"You will. When you do, it'll be because you were

strong enough to fight through that fire, heal from debilitating injuries and be the one to take her down."

He lowered her to the bed and straightened her pillow and bedsheets. Once it was neat again, he tucked her in and smoothed the hair out of her face. He wished he could do more to soothe her, but he would have to take baby steps until she was sure she could trust him again. He trailed his hand down her arm and turned toward his bed, but she grasped his hand tightly and wouldn't let go.

"What do you need, Min?"

"Sleep. I haven't slept in a year, but I need…"

Her words died away, but Roman didn't need her to finish. He knew what she needed. Comfort. Someone to hold her and tell her she would survive this and have a chance at a new life. He could be that person for her right now. All that mattered to him was offering her a safe place to sleep, be it in an armored encampment or his arms.

Roman squeezed her hand and let it drop, then grabbed a blanket off his bed. He settled in behind her and hugged her tightly to his chest before he pulled the blanket over himself. She was under the covers, and he was on top, ensuring there was no miscommunication about what was occurring.

Her sigh of contentment brought tears to his eyes as she tugged his forearm over her and held on for dear life. "I missed you, Roman. I'm still mad at you, but I missed you more than I ever thought possible."

A smile lifted his lips, and he was glad she couldn't see him. "I know part of the feeling I carried every day during my search was you calling out to me. We've been connected for years, and the miles between us couldn't change that. You needed me, and I was going to find you. That's all there was to it."

"Even though I'm still mad, I'm glad you did."

Roman's chuckle filled the silent room before he pressed his nose to the back of her head and inhaled deeply. "I'll take mad as long as you're in my universe again, Wilhelmina August."

He kept his arm tightly wrapped around her middle until her grasp on his wrist loosened and her breathing evened out. Roman couldn't fall asleep, though. His mind kept turning over the little bit of information she'd shared in the car. She sent a message that he never got. If he had, he could have stopped the fire and the escape of The Miss, the right-hand woman of The Madame. He wanted to know why he didn't get it and who stopped it, more than she did. His mind's eye showed her limping into the bathroom earlier, and he corrected himself. No one wanted to know why he didn't get the message to rescue her more than she did. He would figure it out, and then he would prove to her that he didn't abandon her. She abandoned him.

MINA WAS ITCHING to see the bunker. If it held the equipment to help her find The Madame, she wanted to be down there now. The last thing she wanted to do was sit across from Roman and eat breakfast while they pretended that they hadn't been wrapped around each other when they woke this morning. She didn't want to admit to herself that waking up that way had been a dream of hers for years.

If she were honest with herself, she was embarrassed. She had shown weakness to someone who had always seen her as strong and unbreakable. If anyone else had been the one holding her last night, she could have separated the agent from the vulnerable woman, but not with Roman.

"Stop." He reached over and grasped her hand. When she looked down, she had managed to push her food around into one big pile but never put any in her mouth.

"I'm sorry," she whispered, lowering her fork to the plate.

"Don't be sorry. And don't be embarrassed about last night."

Mina let out a sarcastic huff that she wanted to be laughter, but she never got there. "Easy for you to say. You aren't me."

His finger lifted her chin until she made eye contact with him. "That isn't easy for me to say. I know how I would feel if the shoe were on the other foot. I'm an agent. They try to train the emotions out of us, but we're still human at the end of the day. Sometimes, when those emotions get to be too much, we need an outlet. You could find worse ways to deal with it than asking a friend for comfort, especially after being on your own for so long."

"I suppose you're right," Mina admitted, though it almost killed her to do so. She picked at the eggs again, finally taking a bite and washing it down with coffee. She should have been starving, but she was in too much pain after escaping through the woods. She would never tell him that, though. He'd insist she stay up here and rest rather than get to work. He didn't understand that she had to be the one to figure out where The Madame was hiding. If she didn't, she'd never be able to move on with her life.

Roman had gone back to eating, and she watched him from under her brows, taking time to notice him for the first time since he'd found her. He was always a big man, fit, handsome and rugged, but he'd changed since she saw him a year ago. There wasn't an ounce of fat on him anymore. He was all muscle and hard lines, yet when he was holding her last night, he was soft against her back. She wondered how it was possible that the man before her in his black T-shirt, stretched tightly across his hard, sinewy chest, could evoke the feeling of comfort from within her so easily.

"You've lost weight."

"Gained five, actually," he said around a piece of bacon he'd just popped in his mouth.

"Not in fat, Roman. Did you stop eating and do nothing but work out?"

"If I wasn't searching for you, then yeah. Basically, I searched for you for twelve hours, worked out for two and then went back to work."

"Why?" She needed to appease her curiosity, but she suspected it might end up being like that saying about the cat.

He lifted his head and held her gaze when he answered. "The two *P*s, punishment and preparation. Punishment for not getting to you fast enough and preparation for when I found you. My gut told me you were going to need the third *P*."

"Protection," they said at the same time.

"You didn't need to punish yourself for anything, Roman."

"I did, though. I let my partner down, regardless of the circumstances, the how or the why. You can sure as hell count on me this time around. I won't let you down."

"Didn't they put you on another case?" she asked when it filtered through her brain what he'd said his schedule had been for the last year.

"You were my case. The FBI wanted their agent found. My first task was to find out if The Madame had you. Once I learned she was looking for you, too, I knew you'd escaped and were on the run. Trying to track down someone as well trained as you are made it an interesting assignment."

"And you're sure that SAC Moore doesn't know that you've located me?"

He nodded while he swallowed a bite of eggs. "I'm

sure. I got the lead on you through a source that has nothing to do with the bureau."

"Every source has to do with the bureau, Roman," she said with a brow raised.

He matched her brow before he answered. "Cal is discreet."

"Wait, Cal found me?"

"Cal has equipment that can do more underground than I can above ground. I didn't want the SAC to know when I found you. I wanted to get to you first to be sure whatever happened next was your decision and not the government's."

"Thank you. I know what would have happened if the SAC had found me. I probably owe you my life, whether it's because I'm not six feet under or locked in a room for years. Either way, I appreciate that you thought of me and not your career. You know it's over now, right?"

"Oh, yeah," he agreed with a toss of his head. "Jobs come and go, but partners are forever." Before she could respond, he pointed at her plate. "Are you done eating? Cal should be ready for us."

Mina's heart raced at the thought of getting inside that bunker, outpacing the pounding that it had been doing after Roman hit her with the partners forever thing. She wanted to tell him she felt the same way, but she held her tongue because now was not the time or the place. There would probably never be a time or a place, but Mina couldn't worry herself with that right now. She had a Madame to find, and he was dangling the key to the search.

"I'm full." She picked up her coffee mug. "Let's get to work."

Chapter Eight

The workspace Cal had nicknamed The Bunker was only accessible from three places on the property: Cal's room, Roman's room and a hidden trap door that came out on the back side of the farthest cabin. That was only an exit, which meant if you left via the tunnel, you'd better be sure you were never coming back. When Roman had helped Mina down the ladder and into the room, he saw the relief in her eyes. She finally had everything she needed to find The Madame and bring her down.

His focus should be on finding the guys who hurt her and making them pay. It wasn't. All his focus was on her. How soft she was snuggled up against him all night, and how good it felt to wrap her up in his arms and not let her go. His heart hurt inside his chest every time she trembled in her sleep, but then soared when a squeeze from his arms had her relaxing back into him. Mina might be an FBI agent, but last night, she was also a woman with vulnerabilities. Those vulnerabilities were partly his fault, and he warred with himself over hiding her away until

The Madame was found or helping Mina be the one to find the woman. He knew she didn't want protection, but she also couldn't see how much danger she was facing. It was his job to make sure she was protected, whether she liked it or not. She wouldn't like it, but the guilt that swamped him every time she took a step would allow for nothing else.

The Madame couldn't wait. They had to stop her before she hurt more women and destroyed more people's lives. He would take an exorbitant amount of pleasure in bringing her in and then letting Mina have a little alone time with her. A smile quirked Roman's lips. He would pay good money to watch that exchange on a CCTV.

Mina had done an initial glance over the equipment, but now she spun toward him with fire in her eyes. "Are you ever going to tell me why you weren't there the night of the fire, or are you just going to keep pretending it didn't happen?"

"That's not what I'm doing," he assured her. "I didn't want to split your focus now that you have the chance to find your target."

"Trust me when I say my focus is already split. Please, do tell." She motioned at him with a flourish, and he had to bite back a laugh.

The hatch opened to their left, and they both had their guns pointed at it before they took a breath. Roman lowered his gun when he recognized the pair of boots coming down the ladder. He pressed Mina's toward the floor with his hand.

"Wow, you two are jumpier than spit on a skillet," Cal said, hopping down off the ladder.

"You could have announced yourself," Roman said, tucking his gun back in his shoulder harness.

"The risk of getting shot was worth that display of FBI greatness," Cal said, punching him on the shoulder. "What do you think of my setup?" he asked Mina as he turned to her.

"Top-of-the-line everything," she agreed. "I haven't had a chance to start searching yet, but I should have everything I need now to find The Madame."

"Did I interrupt something?" Cal asked, glancing between them.

Roman lowered himself to a chair and braced his hands on his knees. "I was just about to explain why I didn't respond to her message the night of the fire. You may as well stay. I'm done with the FBI at this point, so telling a civilian about a case can't hurt my career."

Mina sat down abruptly and stuck her left leg out to keep pressure off it. She was hurting, and Roman wished there was something he could do to help her. All he could do was help her find The Madame and put the woman behind bars. Only then would it be safe for her to see a doctor again.

"I don't know what happened, Min. After you met me the night before to tell me something was going down, I gathered the team. We were ready and waiting to go in, but I never heard another word. I sent two messages to you via the app but got no response, so I waited as agreed upon at the beginning of the mission. My gut told me something was off, but I had to trust my partner. I should have at least done some recon around the house rather than wait up on that hill," he growled, squeezing his knees with his fingers.

Mina and Cal were silent, as though they were processing what he said. Finally, Mina responded. "If what you say is true, then you followed protocol and our agreed upon terms, Roman. What I don't understand is how you never got the message. I sent it right before I was…accosted," she said, the last word coming out as a cough. Roman could tell she was trying to hold it together.

Cal spoke to Mina. "How did the fire start? Do you remember?"

Roman recovered and pointed at his brother. "We wondered the same thing. It didn't make any sense that The Madame would burn down the house."

"Unless she'd been compromised," Mina answered.

"Had you compromised her?" Roman asked, his eyes wide.

Mina gave him a finger gun. "Only in the sense that The Miss and The Madame figured out I was an undercover agent."

A word fell from Roman's lips that had him smiling sheepishly at Min. She hated profanity, but, in this case, it applied. "We didn't know the SOS was because you were compromised."

"There would be no way for you to know that if you hadn't gotten the other messages. The panic button just tells you to send help."

"I didn't hear from you at our agreed upon time that night, so I assumed that it was taking longer for you to get whatever evidence you'd referred to the night before. In the meantime, I activated the team. Something in my gut said to be ready, so we waited until it was a full two hours past your check-in time."

"She missed a check-in time, and you didn't go in?" Cal asked. His stunned tone had Roman bristling.

"It wasn't that unusual for her to miss a check-in, Cal. If she was busy with the house, sometimes it would be two or three hours later. We were in a rhythm, and I was used to that, but this time, something was off. I should have trusted my gut."

"None of that," Cal said with authority. "As far as you were concerned, she had the tools she needed to reach you if there was a problem. You had no way to know she was out of commission if the message didn't come through."

"He's right," Mina whispered. "As hard as that is for me to admit. I used my anger toward you the last year to keep myself alive, but I never took the time to consider that you may not have gotten the message. My ego about my coding skills was too big, and I was convinced the app had no weaknesses."

"Everything has a weakness," Cal said with conviction.

"That's what I was starting to think by hour two," Roman agreed, standing and starting to pace. "I pulled four guys together, and we were going to approach the house. As we stood on the hill preparing, we saw the flames light up the sky. I lost my ever-loving mind and just ran for the house, the rest of the team hot on my tail. Then the SOS message came through, and I knew you were still inside but all you could do was push a button."

Roman watched Mina's elegant neck bob as she swallowed hard. She leaned in a bit closer, and he did, too, waiting for her to drop something else on him that would destroy him as both an agent and a man.

"I tried to send a message through the app first because I thought I'd have time to get to you." She shook her head and bit her lip for a moment. "I thought it sent. I was heading for the back door to rendezvous with you when they grabbed me."

"Thank God you saw those flames," Cal said, squeezing Roman's shoulder, knowing he needed a moment.

"By the time you saw the flames, The Miss was long gone," she whispered, her words swallowed by the terror in the room. It rolled off her in waves, and Roman wanted to take her in his arms and comfort her, but he couldn't. His guilt wouldn't allow him to show weakness in front of her or his brother. "I was dragging myself to the window with the plan to throw myself out when I found the phone. They'd kicked it under the dresser before they tortured me. I remember hitting the SOS button, but I don't remember anything after that until I woke up after surgery."

Roman remembered. He remembered it all. The smoke and the sound of crackling as the flames licked their way up the side of the house. A shiver went through him, and he coughed to force the images away from his mind.

"So, the SOS message went through, but not the original message. I wonder why?" Roman asked, trying to make sense of the whole thing.

"The SOS wasn't a message. It had different coding. If I hit that button, it just sent an alarm to your phone. They wouldn't have had the inside ability to stop it."

"How did you cover who Roman was?"

"I was a client," Roman answered his brother, reaching out and grabbing Mina's hand to squeeze it.

Mina didn't let go of his hand when she spoke. "The first message said, 'There's a change in plans. Be ready in fifteen minutes. We will bring your date to the agreed upon meeting spot.'"

"You were made, and he needed to get the team ready, and you'd meet up with him in fifteen?" Cal asked, and they both nodded. "Was there any way they could have known that he wasn't a client?"

Mina shook her head. "No. There were so many clients that it was easy to hide him as one without raising anyone's suspicions. My job was to make the dates and organize the girls. The Miss never got involved as long as the money was coming in and the girls were going out."

"They were going to stop any message you sent. It didn't matter what it was," Cal assured her.

"If I had just hit the SOS button the first time," Mina said, staring at the floor.

Roman noticed a tremor go through her, and he squeezed her hand again. "No, don't do that. You did exactly what we agreed upon as step one. Storming the place unprepared could have resulted in death for anyone in that house. That's why we decided to avoid it at all costs. You know that."

"He's right. You can't go back and change things, but we can go forward by finding The Madame."

"That's going to be difficult," she said, a shake of her head barely noticeable other than her hair swaying slightly. "They started the fire and thought I'd burn along with the evidence. The evidence burned, but I didn't. To be honest, I don't even know how I got out alive. I don't remember much other than hitting that SOS button."

"The first floor was already engulfed when we got there," Roman explained. "There was no way to get up the stairs. I found a ladder discarded by the garage, but it wasn't tall enough to reach your window. All I could do was break the glass and get fresh air into the room, which was filled with smoke but hadn't started burning yet."

"I keep trying to remember, Roman. Sometimes I see eyes before the moment is gone."

His eyes. Mina probably remembered his scared, pained, worried eyes gazing down at her and praying she was still alive when the firefighters arrived.

"When I saw how much smoke there was, I couldn't wait. I used the ladder and then the trees until I was able to hoist myself through the window. You were already in bad shape. I carried you to the window and started breathing for you until the firefighters arrived. They got us out, but not before you were nearly dead from smoke inhalation."

"Some days, I wish the smoke had taken me, Roman."

"Don't say that, Mina," Roman insisted, his fists clenching. "Don't say that ever again."

The look she gave him was one he had never seen before, and he had no idea how to read what it meant.

"You didn't let me finish."

Cal chuckled, and so did Roman, her words lifting his lips into a sheepish smile. "You're right. My bad."

"I was going to say, 'and then I remember The Madame is still out there.' It's still my job to stop her. It'll be my last job with the bureau, but I will close this case."

"Mina, there's no reason you can't keep working—"

Mina cut him off with a wave of her hand in the air. "I need to dig into the coding on the app. Is it still active?"

"Yes. The SAC wanted it left online in case you tried to contact us via the app."

Cal glanced between them. "Is it risky to dig into the app now? Will that tip off The Madame that you're back online?"

"Remember, I coded it." She shrugged and motioned at the computer panel. "I wrote a backdoor into the code that only I know is there. Even FBI coders won't find it, which means neither will The Madame's. All I need is a computer and a few hours to get into the information I saved there."

"I have a computer, and you have the skills," Cal said. "It's time to end this nightmare for both of you."

"Do I have a choice?"

"You always have a choice, Mina," Roman said. "We can always go back to Minneapolis and let the SAC deal with it."

She was silent for so long he was convinced she would change her mind about finding The Madame alone. "No. If I make that choice, I could get a whole lot of innocent people killed. In this case, I don't have a choice. I have to suck it up and do what needs to be done."

"There's my girl." Roman ran his finger down her cheek and offered her a wink.

He stepped back while Cal walked Mina through the particulars of his computer system. The Secure One computers were vastly different from the ones she used at the FBI. Roman stood behind them, his thoughts forcing him back to that house with the flames licking around them and the woman he was supposed to protect almost dead in his arms. The memories always left his stomach swirling with how close he came to losing her.

"If you need anything," Cal said, "hit this button, and I'll head back down." He pointed at a black button on the console. "We'll regroup after you've had some time to work on the app."

"Regroup?" Mina asked, and Cal squeezed her shoulder.

"You might not have the FBI behind you anymore, but you still have my men and me. When you have your next course of action, we'll be here to initiate it."

Cal shook Roman's hand and then climbed the ladder, closed the hatch and spun the lock.

"He's something else," Mina said, her hands poised over the keyboard.

"He won't let anyone hurt us here. Family looks after family every time. You're safe. Get to work."

With a grin, her fingers started tapping the keyboard.

MINA'S FINGERS FLEW as she searched the app's code for any breadcrumbs she could use to ferret out The Madame's identity. Too bad she couldn't keep her mind on her work. The picture Roman painted of that night was dark and ugly, but the look in his eyes when he spoke was what did the most damage to her heart. His retelling of having to breathe for her just to keep her alive would remain with her forever. She never wanted him to see her like that. Like this. Weak. Broken. Damaged. She was his partner, and she was supposed to be as strong as he was. She wasn't anymore. She never would be again.

Now she knew they were his eyes that she kept seeing in her dreams. No, in her memories. Her dreams had nothing as comforting as Roman's eyes starring in them. They had nothing but pain and terror. They held the eyes of all the girls she let down in the house that night. Those flashes she'd been getting were memories, and now, thanks to Roman, she could separate the two.

She was so busy thinking about the past that she almost missed what was right in front of her. Her hands fell away from the keyboard on a gasp. Roman, who had been pacing the room for the last hour, was by her side in two steps.

"Did you find something?"

"No." Her head shook as she stared up into the face that had saved her that night. "You said," she swallowed back the fear and forced herself to be the federal agent she'd always been with him. "You said the first floor was already engulfed by the time you got there. Did you get everyone else out? No one was killed or hurt?"

She noticed his slight grimace even in its brevity. "We got everyone, yes."

"Did you get Marlise?"

"Yes." Mina took note of his heavy sigh and

waited him out. There was more to the story. His second sigh told her she was about to get it. "We found Marlise overcome by smoke less than two steps from the front door. There was no one else in the house." He motioned at the computer monitor in front of her. "How much longer before you get to that backdoor?"

"Roman." Her tone was sharp, and he snapped his attention back to her. "Was she hurt?"

He knelt in front of her with his hand on her knee. "Yes. By the time we found her, the fire had spread to where she'd collapsed, and she suffered significant burns to her face, neck and left arm."

"They punished her for warning me, didn't they?" Mina asked with her forehead resting on the table where she'd dropped it.

Roman lifted her chin and stroked the hair back off her face and behind her ear. "Min, listen, nothing that happened that night was your fault."

"Of course it was, Roman. If we hadn't gone in and tried to topple The Madame's empire, Marlise wouldn't be scarred."

"No, she'd probably be dead," he whispered as a reminder. "You do remember the river drownings around the country?"

"Yes, that started about six months into our assignment, but Red Rye doesn't have a river." Mina was confused by his train of thought.

"No, and that's what led the Kansas office to wonder if the towns that had a river also had a house like Red Rye."

"Have there been more drownings since the fire?"

"No, and Kansas thought they could connect those murders to The Madame. Especially since the girls who drowned were scrubbed clean of any identity."

"Just like the girls in the Red Rye house."

"Exactly. Kansas is still working it, but they don't have much to go on other than girls with no identity showing up in random rivers across the country. They're never found in a big river in a big city. It doesn't make any sense."

"It does, though. If those girls are from a house like Red Rye, it wouldn't take much for The Miss's guards to load a woman into a vehicle and drop her in a random river. I'm not saying that's what they're doing, but we have to consider it as a possibility."

"That's true, but they could still be unrelated. It's unlikely considering the girls have no traceable identity, but we can't know for sure until we find The Madame." He pointed at the computer in front of her. "If you want to avenge Marlise, that's how you get the job done. Find the information we need to bury The Madame and all her minions."

Mina's head nod was sharp, and she put her hands back on the keyboard, her fingers flying again. Her mind flew to the voices, faces and secrets she'd come to know during the time she'd been part of The Madame's organization. Had she kept girls alive when she was undercover? Why couldn't she remember what she'd learned before the fire?

Without taking her fingers off the keyboard or

looking at him, for that matter, Mina spoke. "You said I met you the night before the fire to update you. What did I tell you?"

"That you were close to a break in the case, and that's why I got the team ready for the next night. You said you were meeting with someone the next day who would break the case wide open, but you couldn't give me more than that at the time."

Mina's fingers stopped moving for a moment while she laughed. "And you let me go back to the house with so few details about what the break was? That doesn't sound like you, Jacobs."

His shrug was barely there when he paused by the monitor. "I trusted you. You were the one calling the shots. I was there to support you and feed you information from the outside, but I had to rely on you to get the dirty details of the operation. When we met that night, you were vibrating with excitement, and I'd seen you that way before. You were close to a break, and you assured me you were only days away from knowing who The Madame was and the house of cards was going to fall."

"Why can't I remember!" She meant it to be a question, but it came out as an ugly, guttural exclamation. She rubbed her hands over her face and leaned her elbows on the desk, her face in her hands. "The information is sitting on my tongue, but my brain feels disconnected from it. I can't spit it out, and I don't understand why."

"Min, you were given Special K. That's why you can't remember."

Her hands fell away, and she glared at him. "Ketamine makes you forget the time you're under the drug's control, not days before that."

"If you hadn't run out of the hospital before being properly treated, you would have heard the doctor tell us that you had mild edema around your brain on the CT scan. You were punched, or you hit your head on something a few hours before we found you."

A flash of memory hit her, and she shivered. "They tortured me, Roman." She rubbed her temple and sighed. "I get bits and pieces of memories. Flashes, if you will. It's frustrating, but maybe that means I'll remember more soon. I have to, or we're never going to end this manhunt The Madame has put out on me."

Roman walked behind her and started massaging her shoulders. The sensation shouldn't have been erotic, but parts of her that had been dead for years came to life at his touch. Heat roared through her to all the places she hadn't even thought about in over a year. Now, she had to force herself not to think about them when in close quarters with her partner.

"Then we get to work. We work the case as we know it and follow the leads where they take us. We go back to the start and do what we always did. We problem solve. We were partners for so many years because we solved cases, Mina. That's the only reason the bureau never broke us up. Let's do that now and prove to them we can do it again."

"The Gruesome Twosome."

Roman laughed, and her heart soared to hear his laughter again.

"It's been too long since I've heard you say that, Min," he whispered, squeezing her shoulders. "God, it's so good to have you with me again."

"I won't be for long if we don't make The Madame show her face in the light of day. We go back to the start and work the case," she repeated, her fingers on the keyboard again. "We'll follow the leads."

She typed at lightning speed while he kept massaging her shoulders. "That's my girl. Head in the game."

A shiver went through her again. She could only dream about being Roman's girl. When they finished following the leads and solved the case, their partnership would also end. Being chased by men determined to kill her evoked emotions she knew how to cope with and use to her advantage. Losing the one person who had been a constant in her life for so many years while knowing he was living his life with some other woman, she didn't. In the end, if The Madame didn't kill her, losing Roman would.

Chapter Nine

Roman set a plate down in front of Mina. "Eat this."

She picked up the sandwich without taking her eyes off the screen, took a bite and went right back to typing, all without missing a keystroke. Roman had been watching her work for the last two hours and had never felt more useless. His hands were tied until she found something. Until they had a direction to go, all he could do was wait. It hadn't happened and not for lack of trying, either. He could see and feel how frustrated she was today. Breaking into the backdoor of her program was arduous, which she'd done by design. If it took her this long to get into the app's backdoor, it would take someone unfamiliar with it days, weeks or, hopefully, forever.

It was the frustration of not being able to remember the information she thought was in her mind that was bothering her the most, though. He could see it in her eyes when she asked about Marlise. Chances were good that she'd been chewing over Marlise being hurt in the fire since she asked him about it. He wished he had comforting words for her, but the truth was what it was. Marlise was mixed up with The Madame, and that was a dangerous game to play.

"Did you know that the name Marlise means *wished for child* in Hebrew?" she asked after swallowing a bite of her sandwich.

"I didn't," Roman admitted, leaning against the wall with his arms crossed over his chest. He was going for relaxed so she would too, but he knew that would never happen. Not until they were free of the threat coming at them.

"Marlise used to say it as part of a joke she'd make about herself. Her parents surrendered her at a shelter when she was two days old. She would say, 'More like my name meant *wish this child would disappear.*'" She stopped speaking then. Roman could hear the tears in her voice as she choked up. She cleared her throat and went on. "I do remember worrying every day that she was going to disappear."

"She's okay, Min," he promised, squeezing her shoulders. "The person we were most worried about was you." This time, it was Roman's turn to clear his throat. The emotions of finding her alive kept hitting him in all the places he couldn't protect. The thought that he might never have found her was the second of the one-two punches. "I'm still reeling from the fact that I found you, Mina. God, you don't know—" He stopped speaking rather than make a fool of himself.

"I don't know what?" she asked, her hands going still on the keyboard and her body stiffening.

Roman tilted his head to the ceiling and took a

deep breath. "You don't know how many nights I laid awake wondering if you were dead or alive. You don't know how many times I hit the punching bag at the gym out of frustration and terror. You don't know how every time my phone rang, I begged the universe to let it be you. It never was, Min. It never was."

Her left hand came up to cover his right hand on her shoulder. "I didn't know who to trust, Roman. I wasn't just trying to keep myself alive. I was trying to keep the girls who were trapped by The Madame alive, too. They weren't there by their own free will."

She stood up instantly and turned, falling into him until he steadied her. "Some of those girls were bought and paid for, Roman!"

"Slow down, Mina. Tell me what you mean."

"Sex trafficking. That's how The Madame gets the girls."

"We interviewed Marlise, and she never indicated anything to do with sex trafficking."

She grasped her head and twined her fingers in her hair. "I didn't mention it at any time over the year I was undercover that the girls weren't there by choice?"

"No," he promised, his head shaking. "When you briefed us, you indicated the girls were there by choice, though they were hesitant and skittish when they first arrived. They wouldn't talk to you about how they got to Red Rye, but we chalked that up to nerves about the escort service. That said, when the fire happened, you were just getting to the point where The Miss was pulling you deeper into the organization."

"The Miss was The Madame's right-hand woman in Red Rye, but only Red Rye."

"Only Red Rye?" Roman asked on a brow lift.

"Yes… My God, Roman, I remember now. There were other houses full of girls!"

"You told me that when we met the day before the fire," Roman agreed. "If you remember, that's why the SAC initially sent you into the Red Rye house. He wanted you to find out if there were other houses and if sex trafficking was part of the operation. The app was just a convenient way to keep you there until you were indispensable to the organization."

"The FBI knows what cities the other houses were in?" she asked and he nodded.

"Those houses were raided and the women were rescued, but The Madame still escaped capture."

"That's good," Min said with a satisfied nod, "but The Miss didn't know there were other houses until the day before the fire. She wasn't happy because she thought she was leading the charge for The Madame and that the Red Rye house was the beginning of something big."

"Finding out that she was just a smaller part of something bigger made her angry?" he asked, as he waited for her to sort out her thoughts.

Her head nodded as her eyes roamed back and forth as though she were searching her mind for the information. "That was the vibe I got when I overheard her talking to someone on the phone. I don't know if it was The Madame or someone else. I remember now. I was afraid I'd get caught eavesdropping by a guard, so I couldn't hang around to find out who she was talking to."

"Either The Madame kept her in the dark, or she didn't trust her completely yet."

"Could be," she agreed. "Or it could be that there was a Miss at every house, but none of them knew the others existed. You said she was long gone by the time you got there that night?" Mina asked and was rewarded with a nod. She lowered herself back to her chair, and her shoulders slumped. "I remember that I made daily logs on the app. If I can access those, that'll help us unravel the case."

Roman knelt next to her and forced himself not to get lost in her eyes. He'd spend all day gazing into those big, beautiful brown globes if time allowed, but it didn't. He had to concentrate on getting her through this. Only then could he finally let go of the guilt eating him alive and try to find a new kind of normal, even if it wasn't with the FBI…or Mina. "I was always very uncomfortable with the idea of you keeping notes on the app, but the SAC backed you, so I was overruled. Do you think The Miss found your notes?"

"Impossible. I could barely hack it, and I made the app. They figured out who I was some other way."

Roman stood up and motioned for her to continue. She typed and ate for another fifteen minutes before her hands stilled on the keyboard. "I'm in," she said on a breath before her fingers picked up their rhythm again.

His heart raced at the thought that they might finally learn what happened that night. How did The Madame know Min was a plant? They had crafted her persona right down to the last detail of her life. She didn't even look like the woman he knew the day she walked into that house and applied for a job.

"What?" She leaned forward and stared at the computer screen, opening another program and pasting something into a search bar there, pausing while it computed. "See this?" she asked, pointing at the screen.

"It looks like an IP address," Roman said, noting the way the numbers were formatted.

"It is. An IP address from the city manager's office in Red Rye."

"Liam Albrecht?" he asked, his mind trying to follow the trail. "We know he was never involved with the house. The FBI vetted everyone in the local government there."

"I don't know what to say, except that's the IP address that stopped my first message from going out."

"Wait, what?" he asked, his head tipping further in confusion. "Why would the city manager stop your message from going out?"

"I don't know. The second question is, why didn't they use a VPN to hide their activity?" Roman could see the confusion in her eyes.

"Maybe they did…"

Her brow lifted as she stared at the screen. "You mean someone used the IP address for the city manager as camouflage?"

"It's possible. Unusual, but possible."

"We have to assume two scenarios for now. The first is that Liam Albrecht had something to do with the house, and the second is someone else is trying to pin it on him by using his IP address."

"Agreed."

Min stared at the screen while rubbing her forehead. When her hand dropped, her shoulders squared with determination. "I need to talk to Marlise."

"Impossible. We can't leave this compound until we have more information, Mina."

"Then we bring her here."

Roman noted that her words were final, but he wasn't done with the conversation.

"If we make a move on Marlise, we lead The Madame right to our door. You know she's got the girl under surveillance."

"She's not in custody? Roman! You said she was safe!"

He curled his hand around hers and held it lightly, letting her know he was there for her without words. "I know you're scared, but we couldn't force her into custody, Min. She has rights. She refused to talk to us about what went on in Red Rye. She told the SAC she would only talk to you."

"Do we know where Marlise is?" she asked from between clenched teeth.

"She's in St. Paul, and she has an FBI agent assigned for her protection when she goes out. It was hard enough to convince her she needed that, much less convince her to live under the roof of the FBI."

"Get her here, Roman. She holds the key to unlocking my memory. I know it. My gut is telling me she's the key."

"I don't think that's a good idea. I'm certain The Madame has her under surveillance. She'd be dumb not to with what that girl knows. We try to snatch her, and we lead everyone to Secure One's door."

"Fine. I'll go to Marlise. Move out of my way, Jacobs. I don't need your permission to leave here."

Her voice was filled with righteous anger and determination. Roman allowed himself a moment to relish being in the presence of that woman again.

He grasped her upper arms and held her gaze, fierce as it was. "You're correct, but I need you alive, so you can forget about going out there alone. Let me talk to Cal and see what our options are, okay? If we can bring Marlise here safely, we will. You have to give me a little bit of time to do it right, though. We can't jump into a fire again unprepared. We might not make it out alive this time."

She didn't move or say anything for thirty seconds. Roman could see in her eyes the battle she fought to accept her limitations and agree to his terms. He wished things weren't always so hard for her. She deserved a little bit of calm in her life, but he couldn't give it to her, and that bothered him more than it should. That wasn't his job. His job was to keep her alive until the case was resolved. That had always been his one and only job with Mina, even if he wished they could have been more.

"Do you promise you'll talk to Cal?"

"How much longer do you need down here?"

"Hours. I need to follow the trail of this IP address and see if there are any other messages it intercepted. Before I can do that, I need a break. My head hurts, and I need to put my foot up for a few minutes."

Roman was relieved. He could offer her that kind of comfort. Cal's nurse, Selina, had cleaned the wound on her forehead and closed it with Steri-Strips. She had a bruise and a knot on her head that he was sure wasn't helping her sort through all the information filtering through it. Selina suggested that she had a concussion, but Mina had scoffed at that diagnosis. Selina was probably right, though, so he'd encourage Min to rest as often as she could. She was going to need her wits about her the next time they tangled with The Madame.

"I'll help you up the ladder and get you settled, and then I'll find Cal. You'll be waiting when I get back, right?"

"Of course. I don't have a choice. I'm the only one in this for the long haul. If I can't remember what happened in Red Rye and who The Madame is, this is my life forever."

Roman pulled her into him and wrapped his arms around her. "It won't be, and you aren't the only one in it for the long haul. You've controlled my every thought for a year, Mina. Even when I slept, I dreamt of you. We're in this together for the long haul. Do you understand?"

The brush of her cheek against his chest when she nodded almost undid him. The vulnerability in that one motion would be the thing he'd keep in the front of his mind until this was over and Wilhelmina August found her confidence again.

THE AIR WAS crisp as Roman walked toward the lake at the back of the property. October was nearing an end, and in northern Minnesota, that meant cold nights followed by sunny days with a strong breeze. He loved his home state, and he was glad to be back with his family after too many years away. When he stood back and examined his life, Roman didn't recognize it anymore. The only thing he recognized was Mina. He recognized her fighting spirit and "don't give a damn" attitude about her own life when it came to protecting the innocent. He respected her and hated her for it in equal proportions. Their jobs required them both to take risks he couldn't be sure were worth it anymore. In fact, he knew they weren't.

I'll never let you down. I've always got your back.

Roman's promise to his partner rang in his ears as he searched for his brother on the property. He'd promised Mina he'd talk to Cal, and he wasn't going to break another promise to her. If he had to walk to St. Paul and fetch Marlise himself, that's what he would do.

"Good thing there aren't bad guys with guns around here. You'd be dead before you knew what hit you."

"I knew you were there," Roman said, spinning and walking backward a few steps while his brother advanced on him. "I just knew I could take you with one hand without spilling my beer."

"I'd like to see you try," Cal said, laughing.

"I was looking for you." Roman handed him the unopened beer in his hand. "We need to talk."

"Let's go to my office." He motioned forward, and Roman turned to follow him. "Where's Mina?"

"She's resting. I've got Mack looking after her."

"I hope the special agent of the FBI doesn't know there's a mercenary babysitting her. I feel like that wouldn't go over well."

"Do I look dumb?"

"Yes," Cal said without missing a beat.

Roman's bark of laughter echoed across the lake as they walked out onto a dock and settled on a bench at the end.

"Ahh yes, the office created by man and occasionally ruined by man," Roman said, leaning over onto his thighs. Lake Citron was a manmade lake that Cal used for various training exercises with his people, from beach breaching to victim recovery. "It's been too long since I've sat here with you."

"Going on two years," Cal said, popping the top off the bottle of beer and taking a swallow. "You had bigger fish to fry."

They tapped the necks of their bottles together and sat quietly for several minutes, just watching the water ripple across the lake as they neared sundown. Roman had spent the better part of the day in the bunker with Min, and now she needed rest, and he needed answers. He hoped his brother had some.

"Mack asked me if Mina had taken a bullet for you."

"Why would he ask that?" Roman asked curiously, kicking a pebble off the dock into the water.

"He figured that was the reason you were so protective of her. That or you're in love with her."

"Tell Mack to keep his nose out of my business."

"I mean, I can, but then no one would have their nose in your business, most especially you."

Roman's eye roll as he took a drink of beer was his only response.

"I assume you haven't been dating lately. Or should I say at all? Like in the last seven years?"

"Cal?"

"Yeah, Roman?" Cal asked with a smirk.

"Shut up."

"You always were a coward. At least that much hasn't changed." Cal's beer bottle went to his lips, and Roman's brow went up.

"That's a bit like the pot and the kettle. I don't see any women on this compound."

"We're not talking about me, Roman. I haven't been in love with the same woman for seven years and been too afraid to tell her. It wasn't me who spent the last year hunting her down like a man desperate for air. I'm glad you found her, but now you have to break that cardinal rule and tell her how you feel."

"She's my partner and friend, Cal. Nothing more," Roman said before he took a swig of beer.

"Sure, keep telling yourself that. I want you to think about this for a moment, though. What if you had never found her? What if you'd found her dead? What if you never got to tell her what she means to you? Could you live with the idea that you spent six years with her and were never able to call her yours? Think about it. That's all."

Roman had thought about those questions more times in the last year than even he cared to admit. He knew the answers, but knowing and doing were two different things. Right now, he wasn't convinced Mina even trusted him, and maybe she shouldn't. He was the reason she couldn't take a step without intense pain.

"I need help with the case."

"I'm listening."

"I need to procure a package in St. Paul and get it back here without anyone following us."

"A package. I assume you aren't talking about a cat or a dog."

"A woman. Age twenty-seven. Traumatized and scarred from the same fire Min was in."

"What's the end game?"

"Mina swears she holds the key to what happened that night. Marlise was the cook at the house in Red Rye. Mina befriended her early in the investigation, and she's convinced if she can talk to Marlise, everything will snap into focus."

"Do you believe that, too?"

Roman set his empty beer bottle on the dock and leaned in over his knees. "I believe that she believes it."

"Well, that's the most talked around no I've ever heard."

"She developed a special bond with Marlise, and from what she tells me, Marlise is who warned her that she'd been made. It is possible that talking to her could jog Mina's memory, so that alone makes it worth it. Bringing the girl here also takes stress off Mina and helps her relax into the job again."

"All of that is understandable. How hard will it be to obtain the package?"

"Government-protection level difficult."

Cal swore and shook his head, his laughter sarcastic when it fell from his lips. "How in the hell do you think we're going to get her away from witness protection?"

"No, not witness protection. She's living in a government-run facility for victims of crimes. She's been treated for her injuries and her mental and emotional scars. We were hoping to hold on to her long enough to use her as a state's witness, but when Mina didn't show up immediately, Marlise clammed up and refused to talk."

"Does she go to work or school? Can we pick her up somewhere away from home?"

"I checked in on her about a month ago, and she was managing the kitchen at the group home where she lives. She always goes out to pick up orders with a helper who has about fifty pounds of muscle and carries a government badge. Other than that, she doesn't leave the house much except for doctor's appointments."

"Again, with muscle?"

"Yep, but he waits outside."

Cal was silent for a few minutes. "It would be easier to set up a secure line for Mina to talk to her on."

"Easier, yes, but if we bring Marlise here, and she opens up to Mina, it might jog her memory about what happened at the Red Rye house. Marlise might be the catalyst to help us solve this case so both she and Mina can be free."

"It's going to be a tough sell if we don't produce Mina when we pick her up. None of my men are snatching a girl for you, so don't even bother asking. She comes of her own free will or not at all."

"Come on, man," Roman said in disgust. "I don't want you to snatch her. We'll send an image of me, you and Mina. You'll also have a letter from Min explaining to Marlise why she needs to see her. That letter and picture get burned as soon as she's read it. Correct?"

"Understood. This might take me a couple of days to arrange."

"Take your time, but hurry," Roman said, a slight tilt to his lips. "We are running out of it. It's four hours to St. Paul one way. That's a day's travel when you factor in having to lose a tail."

"It's an hour by plane. If I can acquire the package, I can be back here in under four hours."

"I don't trust anyone else with this, Cal."

"Understood, brother. Have Mina get the information ready. If I can make it happen, it'll be tomorrow since it's Friday. Doctors' offices aren't usually open on Saturdays."

Roman's lips tipped up into a smirk when he slapped his brother on the back, stood and headed back to the lodge.

Chapter Ten

"Afternoon, Marlise. How's supper coming along?" Mina had taken to the woman immediately upon her arrival in Red Rye. She was dangerously innocent in a place like this and didn't belong there any more than Mina did. The difference was Mina had the power to give Marlise a better life.

The woman calmly turned on the mixer filled with cookie dough, walked over to Mina and stood shoulder to shoulder with her. "You've been made," she whispered into her ear, rushing a shiver down Mina's spine. "I heard them talking. They know you're an FBI agent. You're not getting out of here alive, Agent August."

Then she calmly walked back to the mixer and finished her work. Mina was a trained agent, so she fought back the panic rising in her throat. Marlise knew her real name, and that was cause to sound the alarm. She snagged a cookie from the pile on the counter and bit into it, casually holding her phone in one hand as though checking her email. She opened *an app and sent a message, then ghosted the app and stuck the phone back in her pocket.*

"Thanks for the cookie, Marlise," Mina said, giving her a wave on her way out of the kitchen. She would sneak out the back door and head to the meetup point with the team Roman was gathering. It was go time, and she had to go.

She had barely made it out of the kitchen before she came face-to-face with The Miss. She plastered on a smile and prepared herself for battle.

"We need you in the boardroom," The Miss said. "Agent August."

Before Mina could react, strong arms grabbed her from behind. She remained calm since her cries would never be heard through the strong hand over her mouth. With her arms trapped behind her, she had no leverage to break free. She kicked out, her foot connecting with something that shot searing pain through her. She screamed on reflex, but the hand wrapped around her mouth kept anyone from hearing her. God, why couldn't she feel her foot? The strong arms dragged her up the stairs, The Miss following them with a gleam in her eye that told Mina she wasn't done with her yet. Mina calmed the panic in her mind and reminded herself she'd sent Roman that message. He'd get to her before The Miss could do much more damage. She just had to stay alive long enough for him to get the team there.

"I always thought you were too good to be true," The Miss hissed, her words laced with venom. "I love

being right." Her arm swung out, and more searing pain engulfed Mina as a scream tore from her throat.

"Mina! Wake up! Come on, baby. You're okay. You're safe here."

Mina's eyes opened as her chest heaved. She stared into Roman's sleepy face. His gaze held fear and uncertainty, and she reached out, caressing his cheek to ground herself. "It happened again, didn't it?"

"If by *it* you mean a nightmare, then yes."

She smiled at his words, even though she wanted to cry from the pain in her foot. She relived the pain every time she had the dream, which was happening more and more frequently now.

"I used to think they were nightmares, but now I know they're more like flashbacks while I'm asleep."

"Your mind is helping you remember when you're in an unconscious state?" he asked, lowering himself to the side of the bed and keeping hold of her hand. She liked that his giant paw swallowed hers. It made her feel safe in a world she knew was anything but safe.

"Something like that," Mina agreed, running her hand over her face. "It's always different parts of my time in the Red Rye house. Tonight, I was dreaming about the minutes after Marlise told me I'd been made."

"Are you sure that's what she meant?"

"Yes, I remember now. She told me I wasn't getting out alive and then called me Agent August."

A curse word fell from Roman's lips that had her raising a brow. "Sorry, but if that was a flashback, then the whole operation was compromised at some point."

She sat up and leaned against the headboard, accepting a bottle of water from him for a drink. "It was real. After she called me Agent August, I took out my phone and sent you the message you never got. As I was headed for the back door to meet up with you, The Miss and one of her goons stopped me. She called me Agent August once her goon had me in a chokehold. I kicked out, and instantly, white-hot pain lanced my foot. The Miss said she knew I was too good to be true and then… I think… Roman, I think she was stabbing me?"

The look on his face told her she was right.

She drank some water and set the bottle back on the table. "I know what happened now." The words were whispered, but they sent a visible chill through Roman. "I can still feel the pain of the knife that went through my shoe and into my foot when I kicked out." She rubbed her left lower calf because she knew better than to touch her foot. "I screamed, but no one could hear me. We were almost to my room when she did it again." The water threatened to come back up, and Mina swallowed several times to keep it down. "Once they got me in my room, they put the knife down and picked up a mallet. Every time I refused to answer a question, they pounded on my foot." Her head fell back to the pillow, and she gulped air just to keep from vomiting at the memories of that time trapped in a room with people who wanted her dead.

"Will you show it to me? I need to understand."

"Show you what?" Mina asked, resting on her elbows to look at him.

"Your foot."

"I don't want to do that."

"I understand that, Min. I know how bad it was when I found you that night. What I need to know is, what is it like now? If we need to run, I have to know if you can, or if I need to cover you."

Her laughter was thin and laced with unrelenting pain. "That depends on the day and the terrain, Jacobs."

"Why do you call me Jacobs whenever you want to put distance between us? If you think I don't notice, you're wrong. I'm here to help you stay alive until we bring down The Madame. That's my only goal, so don't hamper my efforts this early in the game."

Mina's insides quivered at the thought of showing him how broken she was now. Every time she looked at the foot, it reminded her she would never be an agent again, which meant losing Roman as her partner. A mangled heart would be harder to live with than her mangled foot. At least they could remove the mangled foot to get rid of the pain. They couldn't remove her heart.

She brought her knee up, and he grasped her sock, babying it down over her heel. When he pulled it off the toes, Roman stared at it in silence. His hand took hers on instinct.

"How do you even walk, Min?" he asked, his voice a harsh rasp. "You relied on me to be your eyes and ears, and the one time it mattered most, I failed you."

She grabbed angrily at the sock. "This is why I didn't want to show you!" She sucked in a deep breath to steady herself. "I don't want you to feel guilty. This wasn't your fault. You couldn't have stopped it, even if you got the first message."

Roman held her hand to the bed to stop her from putting the sock back on. "Tell me what happened. They couldn't tell us at the hospital because of privacy laws."

"I think you can see what happened with your own eyes."

Her foot was a cobweb of scars from knives and burns. It wasn't burned in the fire that night, but as a torture tactic to get her to reveal what she'd told the FBI about the Red Rye operation. She refused, and her foot had paid the price. Her bones sat at odd angles, and the fifth toe was gone. The doctors had told her it was nearly amputated when she'd arrived and they couldn't reattach it.

"How do you walk on this?"

"Carefully." She uttered the word ruefully, and Roman smiled in appreciation of her attempt to lighten the mood. "I have a brace I wear to support the foot and the muscles. Without it, I wouldn't walk, much less run."

"Did you get that from a doctor?"

"Not exactly." Her answer was vague on purpose, and he stared her down until she relented. "I bought it off the shelf. It works."

"For now," he said, reaching into the drawer by the bedside. He came out with a tube of ointment and held it up. "Cal uses this for his hand that's been injured."

"I noticed he had several high-tech fingers. What happened?"

"A mission gone wrong," Roman said, his lips in a grim line. "Shrapnel nearly destroyed his hand, but they were able to save everything but his two middle fingers. His hand is still sensitive, so he wears the prosthesis to protect it and improve his grip." He held up the tube. "He also uses this to keep the swelling down and ease the pain. Would it be okay to try it on your foot?"

Mina held her hand out for it, and she read the tube before handing it back. "I've heard about it. It's supposed to work great, but I never had access to it."

Roman opened the tube and squirted a ribbon on his hand, but she moved her foot out of the way before he could touch it.

"No." The one word was punctuated with a finger in his chest. "No. You are not touching it."

"I'm not going to hurt you, Mina. I'll be gentle."

She shook her head while she forced tears back

from her eyes. "No. You don't want to touch it. Just...
don't."

He rubbed the ointment between his palms to
warm it but didn't speak. He simply slathered the
ointment across her skin. She closed her eyes so she
didn't have to see his face when he touched her leathery skin and followed the macabre pattern of her
bones that jutted out at unnatural angles. She inhaled
deeply and shook away the pain of knowing one day
she'd lose this man and have to reinvent herself all
over again. And she'd do it. She had to survive the
onslaught of The Madame so she could keep helping women like Marlise.

Roman's touch was light but warm, as though he
wanted to heal her with his hands. Any comfort he
could offer her was welcome. She had suffered for a
year with unrelenting pain in that foot, so she'd take
the five minutes of solace he offered. He tenderly
covered her foot with the sock when he finished rubbing in the ointment and then climbed off the bed.

She listened to him wash his hands, and when he
returned, he carried a bottle of pain reliever. She had
curled into a ball on her side, the blanket pulled up
to her chin, and a lone tear ran down her cheek. She
angrily brushed it away with her blanket.

"Mina, honey, did I hurt you?" When she didn't
answer, he knelt and handed her the medication and
bottle of water. She swallowed the pills, but she
couldn't stop her hand from shaking while she did it.

"You didn't hurt me. I never wanted you to see

my foot, but now that you have, I'm afraid it's going to change everything between us."

"I saw it the night of the fire, Min." He pushed the hair off her sweaty face and trailed a thumb down her cheek. "If I needed more proof that you're the strongest person I know, seeing your foot that night sealed it for me."

She wanted to speak. She wanted to say something smart-alecky or try to downplay it, but after what she'd gone through, all she had left was the truth. "I know I'm not the woman you left the day before the fire."

"You're right," he said, running his hand down her arm to take her hand. "You're twice as strong and twice as beautiful in my eyes. You're also twice as smart. Somehow you managed to stay off the radar for an entire year while dealing with a traumatic injury that has become a permanent disability. I might come off like a bumbling oaf, but I want you to know that I'm proud of you. I know you can hold your own in any fight."

"Not a physical one anymore," she admitted. She rubbed her forehead and avoided eye contact with the man who had just called her beautiful.

"Hey," he whispered. "Would you like to go back to sleep now?"

"No." She shook her head for added emphasis. "I won't sleep now for a bit. I need to let the dream fade away, or I'll be too tense to sleep."

"I have an idea if you're up for it. I know a place

Loyal Readers
FREE BOOKS Voucher

We're giving away THOUSANDS of FREE BOOKS

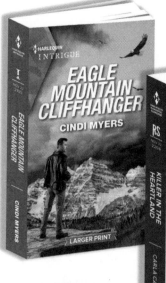

Don't Miss Out! Send for Your Free Books Today!

See Details Inside

Get up to 4
FREE FABULOUS BOOKS
You Love!

To thank you for being a loyal reader we'd like to send you up to 4 FREE BOOKS, absolutely free when you try the Harlequin Reader Service.

Just write "YES" on the Loyal Reader Voucher and we'll send you 2 free books from each series you choose and Free Mystery Gifts, altogether worth over $20.

Try **Harlequin® Romantic Suspense** books featuring heart-racing page-turners with unexpected plot twists and irresistible chemistry that will keep you guessing to the very end.

Try **Harlequin Intrigue® Larger-Print** books featuring action-packed stories that will keep you on the edge of your seat. Solve the crime and deliver justice at all costs.

Or **TRY BOTH** and get 2 books from each series!

Your free books are completely free, even the shipping! If you continue with your subscription, you can look forward to curated monthly shipments of brand-new books from your selected series, always at a discount off the cover price! Plus you can cancel any time.

So don't miss out, return your Loyal Readers Voucher today to get your Free books.

Pam Powers

LOYAL READER
FREE BOOKS VOUCHER

◄ DETACH AND MAIL CARD TODAY! ▼

YES! I Love Reading, please send me up to 4 FREE BOOKS and Free Mystery Gifts from the series I select.

Just write in "YES" on the dotted line below then return this card today and we'll send your free books & gifts asap!

→ YES ←

Which do you prefer?

| ☐ **Harlequin® Romantic Suspense** 240/340 HDL GRS9 | ☐ **Harlequin Intrigue® Larger-Print** 199/399 HDL GRS9 | ☐ **BOTH** 240/340 & 199/399 HDL GRTL |

FIRST NAME | LAST NAME

ADDRESS

APT.# | CITY

STATE/PROV. | ZIP/POSTAL CODE

EMAIL ☐ Please check this box if you would like to receive newsletters and promotional emails from Harlequin Enterprises ULC and its affiliates. You can unsubscribe anytime.

Your Privacy – Your information is being collected by Harlequin Enterprises ULC, operating as Harlequin Reader Service. For a complete summary of the information we collect, how we use this information and to whom it is disclosed, please visit our privacy notice located at https://corporate.harlequin.com/privacy-notice. From time to time we may also exchange your personal information with reputable third parties. If you wish to opt out of this sharing of your personal information, please visit www.readerservice.com/consumerschoice or call 1-800-873-8635. **Notice to California Residents** – Under California law, you have specific rights to control and access your data. For more information on these rights and how toexercise them, visit https://corporate.harlequin.com/california-privacy.

HI/HRS-622-LR_LRV22

© 2022 HARLEQUIN ENTERPRISES ULC
™ and ® are trademarks owned by Harlequin Enterprises ULC. Printed in the U.S.A.

⬥ HARLEQUIN Reader Service — **Here's how it works:**

Accepting your 2 free books and 2 free gifts (gifts valued at approximately $10.00 retail) places you under no obligation to buy anything. You may keep the books and gifts and return the shipping statement marked "cancel." If you do not cancel, approximately one month later we'll send you more books from the series you have chosen, and bill you at our low, subscribers-only discount price. Harlequin® Romantic Suspense books consist of 4 books each month and cost just $5.49 each in the U.S. or $6.24 each in Canada, a savings of at least 12% off the cover price. Harlequin Intrigue® Larger-Print books consist of 6 books each month and cost just $6.49 each in the U.S. or $6.99 each in Canada, a savings of at least 13% off the cover price. It's quite a bargain! Shipping and handling is just 50¢ per book in the U.S. and $1.25 per book in Canada*. You may return any shipment at our expense and cancel at any time by calling the number below — or you may continue to receive monthly shipments at our low, subscribers-only discount price plus shipping and handling.

▲ If offer card is missing write to: Harlequin Reader Service, P.O. Box 1341, Buffalo, NY 14240-8531 or visit www.ReaderService.com ▲

BUSINESS REPLY MAIL

FIRST-CLASS MAIL   PERMIT NO. 717   BUFFALO, NY

POSTAGE WILL BE PAID BY ADDRESSEE

HARLEQUIN READER SERVICE

PO BOX 1341

BUFFALO NY 14240-8571

NO POSTAGE
NECESSARY
IF MAILED
IN THE
UNITED STATES

where you can reach out and touch the stars. Would you like to see it?"

"Is it a long walk?"

"It's a fair way, but we'll take it slow and stop as often as you'd like. I promise once you're out there, the walk will be worth it."

She tossed the covers back with purpose and scooted to the end of the bed. "If you throw in a bottle of Jim Beam, that will make the walk worth it."

"Done," Roman said with a smirk as he grabbed her shoes and brace and set them by the bed.

ROMAN WANTED TO FORGET, but he couldn't. The destruction of her foot was proof that he'd dropped the ball on the one person he never wanted to let suffer. You could hardly call what she was walking on a foot. It was just a mishmash of scarred flesh and bones in places they shouldn't be. There was no fat whatsoever, and it must hurt like hell. She limped along next to him, and he kept his arm around her waist, helping her over the uneven grass.

"The brace I wear keeps me upright, but it doesn't give me stamina," Mina explained, her voice quiet even in the still of the night. "That's what happened in the woods that night. I had miscalculated how far I could go before resting. The woods had more difficult terrain to navigate than I'd anticipated. I should have planned better. I felt safe in Chester and didn't leave on my normal schedule. I was tired and thought a few extra months in one place wasn't a big deal."

Her tone held shame, and Roman hated that she felt anything other than how strong he knew her to be.

"The extra months wouldn't have hurt, except that when I found you, I brought The Madame along behind me. I still won't apologize for tracking you down. How did you even escape the hospital, Mina? I left long enough to take a shower, and there was another FBI guard at your door. You weren't out of surgery twenty-four hours. You had to be in excruciating pain."

Her nod was sharp, and she coughed as though thinking about it still sent her back there. "I was, but that pain would be nothing if The Madame got to me. I wasn't thinking clearly. I was running more on autopilot than anything. At the time, I thought you'd abandoned me in the house, which made me wonder if you were working with The Madame. I knew I couldn't stay there long, but didn't see an escape until the agent they assigned to my door got ill. He took off for the restroom, and I saw a chance. I pulled the IV out and climbed into the wheelchair they'd left in my room. I waited, knowing the nurse would eventually leave the station. Sure enough, they got a code blue on the floor, and off she went. I managed to get to the elevator without seeing the agent again."

"Where did you go from there?"

"I had my bugout bag stashed where I could get to it quickly, along with a car. I managed to get to it, stashed the wheelchair in the back and took off. I found a hotel and laid low for a few days, then moved on until I got far enough away from Red Rye that it was safe to seek medical attention."

"How did you pay for that? Do you have bills outstanding?"

"Some," she answered as the lake came into view. She paused on the next step and sighed. "Look at that view. You were right. It was worth the walk here."

Roman helped her onto the dock, and they walked to the bench, where she lowered herself down. He sat next to her and rested his arm over the back of the bench. He wanted to touch her just to remind himself that she was real and she was here.

"The bureau will cover the bills. You just have to let them know who to pay."

"Maybe," she said. "I'm no longer employed by them, Roman."

He held up his finger until she paused. "Untrue. You're still an active agent of the FBI."

"I won't be for long when they see this foot," she said with a head shake. "I paid cash for almost everything. I had to dip on a couple of more expensive procedures, which I feel bad about, but the person they treated doesn't even exist. I had cash, but I had to make it last."

"Where did you get the money? Certainly not on what we make a month."

Her laughter filled the night sky, and Roman ate up the sound. She was relaxed for a moment, and he wanted more of that for her. "How true that is. Do you remember when my meemaw died a few years ago?"

"I sure do. She was a sweet lady who raised you right."

"I hope she would still think so," she agreed on a faraway sigh. "Once I sold her house and had all her assets together, I put them in a national bank under a fake name that I could access from anywhere in the country. That money kept me alive all these months, so I didn't have to work and risk being found by The Madame."

"Is the money gone now?"

"Not by a longshot. Why do you think I told Cal to protect the Fairlane?"

Her wink nearly did Roman in. He smiled while he tenderly rubbed her neck until goosebumps covered her skin. "Your meemaw would be glad to know she was able to do that for you. Had you stayed, the FBI would have protected you, baby." The endearment slipped out, but Roman was glad when she didn't bristle.

"I didn't know who I could trust, Roman. Everything went so bad so quickly, and I had no choice. If I stayed and trusted the wrong person, I'd be dead."

"If you trusted me, you mean."

Her shrug was heavy under his hand where it rested against her shoulder. "Not just you. I couldn't trust anyone until I knew why no one came to save me that night."

"Did you follow the case in the news?"

"In the beginning, when they were still talking about it on the television, but once it was no longer headline news, I couldn't risk checking the net."

"How did you plan to figure out who to trust then?"

She was silent for so long Roman thought she'd fallen asleep on the bench. When she spoke, she said the very last thing he expected her to say. "I waited to see if you'd find me. You know things about me that no one else in the bureau knows, so I left information behind. If you were looking, you'd know to keep following the clues. I guess it worked because here you are."

She grabbed the bottle of Jim Beam from his hand and took a swallow of it.

"Wait, what?" he asked, leaning forward to make eye contact with her. "You wanted me to find you? How did you know you could trust me?"

"I didn't," she answered without pause. "But I needed help, and I had nowhere to turn. If you found me, I was hoping that it was because you wanted to help me and not kill me."

"Mina," Roman said, but the retching of his stomach halted his words for a moment. When he recovered, he took her hand in his. "The mere idea that you thought I would kill you makes me sick. I wanted to find you because you called out to me, and I heard those cries in my sleep. I spent a year as a raving lunatic trying to find you, and every day that passed, I worried I was going to be too late. When I found a hospital that had treated a 'Rebecca Sweet', it was magic. I figured out you were combining names from our cases to use as aliases, and then I was able to get Cal to help me locate you."

"It was a risk I had to take if I wanted you to find me. My only mistake was not considering that The Madame would likely follow you. I put you in danger by leaving those clues."

"No," Roman said, lifting her chin to hold his gaze. "I knew the possibility was there, but I couldn't let it deter me from finding you. I had to protect you, but I couldn't if I didn't know where you were."

Mina lowered her head to his shoulder and stared out over the lake. "I want this to end," she whispered over the sound of the rippling waves. "I'm so tired."

"I know," he said, resting his cheek on the top of her head. "That's why we're here. To make this end for everyone."

"What did Cal say about Marlise?"

When Roman had returned to the room from meeting with Cal, Mina had been down for the count. Rather than wake her, Roman let her sleep, figuring she could get back to work when she was rested. The woman he used to know could work for days on just a few hours of sleep. The woman in his arms tonight could barely work a few hours before she needed to rest. The pain and terror of the last year had worn her down, and he was worried she'd never be the same again. Who was he kidding? Of course, she'd never be the same again. She carried physical and emotional scars of a mission gone wrong, and he was to blame for that. Touching her foot tonight drove home that he didn't deserve to call her his partner, or anything else for that matter.

"He's working out a plan to fly into St. Paul, pick her up and bring her out here. He hopes to have it accomplished by tomorrow night." He paused and shook his head. "Or rather by late tonight. It's going to be risky."

"How will he convince her to go with him? If I were Marlise, I'd be afraid of a bunch of guys Cal's size coming after me."

Roman chuckled and planted a kiss on the top of her head. That was better than planting one right on her lips like he wanted to. "Cal wants you to write her a coded letter with an image of the three of us together to prove that he knows you. The letter won't be understandable until Cal puts it through a special program to decode it once he's with her. After she reads it, the letter will cease to exist. If that doesn't work, Cal will return without her. He refuses to snatch her and take the heat for that."

"No!" Mina exclaimed, raising her head immediately. "I don't want him to snatch her. That would be traumatizing. I'll add things to the letter that only the two of us would know, so she knows it's me and not The Madame. I wish we had another option, but something inside me tells me this is the only way."

"Then we'll do it," Roman promised, rubbing her

shoulder to relax her. "I'll do whatever I have to do for you to find peace, Mina."

"It's peaceful out here," she said, her hand motioning at the lake before it fell to her lap.

"Cal calls it his office."

"I can see why."

Roman gazed down at the woman in his arms, and hers flicked to his and held there. The brown in her pain-filled eyes melted away in that moment. "Not nearly as gorgeous as you are, Wilhelmina August. You send me. You always have."

"Send you where?"

"Places I shouldn't even be thinking about."

"But you are?"

He let his eyes fill with all the emotions he felt for her, and before she could object, he captured her lips with his. He kissed Min like he was a man without a home. What he meant to keep languid and light, allowing her the chance to break it off, quickly heated when she leaned into him, latching her arms behind his neck and holding on for dear life. She returned his kiss, which told him that she wanted this as much as he did. The kiss held so much pain and promise that Roman worried his heart would pound out of his chest. She tasted of Jim Beam, pain and redemption, but he wasn't convinced he deserved the last one.

He let the kiss end naturally and rested his forehead against hers while they caught their breath. She was the one to speak. "You just broke your cardinal rule, Agent Jacobs."

He traced a finger down her cheek before he buried the same hand in her hair, holding her close to him. "That rule only existed because of you, Agent August. I've wanted to kiss you for seven long years."

"Was it worth the wait?"

Roman noticed her voice was breathy and wanton, which told him his answer mattered to her. "Oh, sweet Mina. I would have waited seven more years for a kiss like we just shared."

"What if I said I didn't want you to wait?"

"Then I'd say this," he answered as his lips lowered to hers, and he kissed her to the crickets' serenade.

Chapter Eleven

Mina's mind and heart were still reeling from the kisses she shared with Roman last night. Her mind was ticking a million miles a minute with thirty-nine tabs open, and none of it made any sense to her. All she could focus on was the feel of his lips against hers. The warmth of his tongue when it pushed through the barrier to dance with hers. He'd whispered that he'd held himself at bay with an iron will for years, but that disappeared the night of the fire. It was replaced with other things. Things like fear. Desperation. Understanding. Learning how quickly something you want can be taken away.

The computer screen in front of her needed her attention, but her mind kept drifting back to Roman and how he'd held her last night. Protective was an understatement. Possessive might begin to cover the feeling. She noticed when she was in his arms the bad dreams stayed away. He kept the nightmares at bay with the length of his warm body pressed the full length of hers. How many times had she wished for the same thing over the last seven years? Too many to count. But not like this. Not on the run and as damaged as she was. Roman wanted the old Mina, but that woman no longer existed in this world.

"What the hell?" she asked the empty room, leaning in closer to the screen. Roman was helping Cal with recon on Marlise while she hacked into Liam Albrecht's office in Red Rye. "Why would he be corresponding with a senator?"

Okay, so maybe it was a senator for the state of Kansas. That would make sense. She opened another tab and typed in Senator Greg Weiss. In seconds, she knew that wasn't the case. Senator Weiss was from the great state of Maine. She read through some of the emails and shrugged.

"They could just be friends." While true, something felt off, so she flipped back to the other tab to type in the two names together just as there was a knock on the hatch.

"It's just me, Min," Roman called.

He climbed down the ladder with Cal following him. Neither of the men looked happy, and that made Mina's heart tick a little bit faster. "What?" she asked them as soon as they were standing in front of her. "Something's wrong."

Roman raised a brow at her, and Cal grinned. "I guess you win," Cal said.

"Win what?" she asked, aggravation clear in her voice.

"I told Cal you'd know something was wrong the

minute you saw us. Listen, Min, there's been a problem in procuring Marlise."

"What kind of problem?" She glanced between the two men, but neither spoke. "Tell me, and don't sugarcoat it."

"She was attacked on the way back from the store outside her house yesterday. They took out her guard and went to town on her, but she fought back."

Mina's heart sank at the news. "That sounds like Marlise. She was always so quiet and meek, but you knew there was anger simmering underneath. Did they take her?"

"No," Roman said, grabbing her hand for comfort. "Her guard came around in time to get in some licks, but he didn't take either of them into custody. The two guys took off, but he couldn't risk leaving Marlise to go after them."

"Where is she now?" Mina asked through clenched teeth.

"At the hospital," Cal supplied. "They beat her up good. She's got a broken arm and nose, busted lip and a concussion, but it could have been much worse."

Mina turned to Roman and grabbed his shirt. "We need to get her out of there. The Madame's men will come for her again."

He wrapped his hand around hers. "We know."

"We have a plan," Cal promised, his voice calm and comforting. "It's still risky, but it's the only option we have now."

"What's the plan?" she asked, easing her grip on

Roman's shirt. "I'll do anything to get her out of there."

"You won't have to do anything," Roman promised. "You'll wait here with Mack while Cal and I go pick her up at the hospital."

"How does that even make sense?" she asked, her gaze bouncing between them. "She's not going to go with two guys she doesn't know if I'm not there."

"You're not going," Roman said firmly. "Regardless, she knows me since I've interviewed her several times. She trusts me where you're concerned, Min. She'll believe I found you on my word alone, especially after this attack."

"Roman," she started to say, but he cut her off.

"Min. I can't lose you again. I can't," he said between clenched teeth.

Cal held his hand up to Roman. "I warned you that she wasn't going to go for this. I have a different plan if you'd like to hear it," he said, addressing Mina.

"It better involve me going to get Marlise."

"It does," Cal said with laughter as Roman glared at him with a death stare. "Safely, of course."

"There is nothing safe about your plan, Cal!"

"Safer than having your partner go rogue again to try and beat us there. Have some respect for her, Roman. She's still an FBI agent. She has every right to participate in something that could save her life, whether you like it or not."

"Where do you get off—"

Mina stepped between the two men before Roman

could start an angry tirade. "Gentlemen. This isn't
helping. I understand both sides here. Trust me. I
get it more than you two combined, but Roman,"
she said, turning to him, "Cal is right. If I'm with
you, we stand a better chance of the mission being
successful. I can convince Marlise to come with us.
I know I can."

She held Roman's gaze and saw in his eyes all
the fear that he'd gone through over the last year.
She hated herself for it, even though she knew it
had been beyond her control. She leaned into him.
"I know you're scared to lose me, but if we get Marlise, we get the answers we need to sort out this tangled web of lies."

Roman sighed and gave a slight nod of his chin.
"You might be right, but I still hate it. I hate putting
you at risk again. Regardless of a disguise, we can't
hide the limp you have on your left foot."

"I have a solution for that," Cal said, and they both
turned back to him. "If we're pulling this caper off as
a medical transport, then you'll both go in as EMTs.
I have access to a cast boot she can wear to hide the
limp. Do you think you can walk in one of those?"

She nodded before he finished speaking. "That's
what I was wearing up until six months ago. It
changes my gait, so I can't run, but walking and
pushing a gurney would be no problem."

"Let me get everything in place then. We're going
in at a shift change, when there are fewer people
to notice us. This is unsanctioned. You both know

you'll lose your badges for pulling her out from under the FBI's nose, right?"

"No choice," Roman said. "I could take Mina in to get the information from Marlise, but the second we walk out that door, Marlise is dead. The Madame will find her, and her goons will kill her. Probably our agent too."

"Agreed," Cal and Mina said in unison. "Anyway, my badge isn't worth the metal it's printed on," Min added.

"I don't care about my badge," Roman said between clenched teeth. "I care about saving people's lives. I don't care what I have to give up to make that happen."

"Then I'll get the plan in place," Cal said on a nod. "To make you feel better, Roman." He stopped talking, dug in his pocket and pulled out two small black phones. He handed one to each of them. "These phones will only communicate with other phones on the circuit. The only other phones are mine and Mack's. If you get separated from the group, hit the star button twice, and you'll turn on the tracker."

"How is that going to keep me safe?" she asked, flipping the phone over twice. "That'll just lead The Madame to me."

"I can trace the phone from here, but no one else can. If you need to ditch it, snap it in half and toss it. But try not to. They're expensive." Mina laughed as he started climbing up the ladder. "Be ready in twenty. You can change clothes on the plane. Mina, I'll have a wig and makeup for you."

When he closed the hatch, Mina spun back to Roman slowly, her face a mask of neutrality. She couldn't show weakness, or he would try to convince her to stay here where she was safe. Any other time she would, but not when it was Marlise they were trying to save.

"I know," he whispered before she could say anything. "I don't like it, but I understand. She's your friend."

"She may have saved my life. She gave me enough warning to see what was coming, and if my message had gone through, none of this would be happening. I owe her the same dedication since it's the bureau's fault she's living this way."

He shook his head, but his smile was more natural when he flashed it at her. "No, Marlise is living this way because she picked sisters over misters."

"What?" Mina asked with confusion.

"She's protecting you, babe. She has been questioned by the FBI extensively, and she refuses to tell them anything. The only person she'll talk to is you."

"But she doesn't even know if I'm alive."

"Exactly. She's still willing to live with an agent tailing her all day, every day on the off chance you are. That means she knows her information will help you find The Madame, and you're the only person she's willing to give it to."

"That sounds like the Marlise I knew," Mina said

with a smile. "Let's go get her so we can end this cat-and-mouse game with The Madame and get on with our lives."

"I couldn't agree more." Roman ducked his head and stole her lips. The kiss was gentle and languid, but Mina used it to say everything to him that her words couldn't.

MINA WAS NERVOUS. The plan was solid, but it was still a risk, and she hadn't done this kind of work for a year, much less on a foot that barely responded to her orders. Thank goodness she had the stretcher to push for balance. Hopefully, the boot fooled anyone watching. The blond wig tied up in a ponytail under her Lakeview Transport Team hat would confuse anyone who knew her, and so would the stage makeup applied to give her a scar that ran down underneath the cloth hospital mask she was wearing. Roman was wearing a disguise too, and all she could do was pray that no one asked them why they were wearing the masks.

"Remember the plan," Roman whispered. "Deviating from it is a death sentence."

She nodded and continued pushing the gurney into the hospital to ride up to the third floor, where Marlise waited. She had a new guard on her, thanks to the first guy sporting a concussion, but they had to rely on Mack to make a disturbance to draw the agent away so they could get Marlise out of there. They would have a matter of minutes to convince

Marlise to go with them. All they could do was hope
that Marlise would agree as soon as she saw Mina's
face. The rest of the plan consisted of getting back
to the ambulance, where Mack would drive them to
the plane parked at a private airport. Cal planned on
wheels up in an hour. That gave them enough time
as long as everything went as planned.

The elevator dinged to signal they'd arrived at the
third floor, and she took a deep breath, glancing at
Roman for the encouragement she knew he'd give
her. She wasn't disappointed. He winked and whispered, "We got this. We've been through far worse."

His words, and the memories of those times,
straightened her spine as the doors slid open. Just
as she pushed the gurney out, they heard shouting in
a hallway across from Marlise's room. Mina grinned
behind her mask as she hurriedly pushed the gurney to room 305. Roman didn't wait for permission.
He threw the door open, and she pushed the gurney
through before he shut it behind him.

Mina lowered her mask. "Marlise, it's me, Mina."

Her friend gasped and brought a shaking hand to
her lips. "You're alive."

"Yes," Mina said, hugging her friend for no more
than a second. "But I won't be for long if we don't
talk. We can't do that here. Will you come with us?
We have a transport ambulance waiting to take us to
a plane and a safe place." She motioned at Roman.
"This is my partner, Agent Jacobs."

"I know Roman," Marlise said shyly. "He never gave up on you, so I didn't either."

Tears flooded Mina's eyes, and she nodded once. "I'm grateful that you both knew me that well. Please, come with us?"

Marlise nodded, and Roman strode over, scooping her up off the bed and onto the gurney before she finished the motion. Mina attached her IV bags to the pole on the gurney and covered her with several blankets. She had to take a steadying breath when she noticed the burn scars over the left side of her friend's body. Guilt lanced her, but she pushed it aside to get the job done.

"I'm putting the straps on just to make it look real. Once we're in the ambulance, we'll take them off," Roman explained, dragging Mina back to their present situation.

"That's okay. I might fall off without them. This arm is a problem." Marlise held up her cast, and Mina frowned before she lifted her mask back to cover her face. "We'll get you medical care once we get somewhere safe. Ready to move?"

Marlise lay back on the stretcher and closed her eyes as though she were sleeping. Mina pulled the door open and looked left and right. There was no one in the hallway. All they had to do was get to the elevators, and they'd be in the clear until the agent realized Marlise was missing.

"Come on, Mack, hold him for us," Roman chanted as they pushed the gurney down the hallway.

Without opening her eyes, Marlise said, "Turn right at the next bend. There's a patient transport elevator for moving patients in beds from the ER and OR. No one will see you waiting for it."

Mina glanced up at Roman, and he nodded, turning the stretcher down the hallway just as she caught sight of an agent walking back to Marlise's room, shaking his head. "We have seconds," she hissed as Roman hit the button. They waited for the elevator, both anxious and chanting "come on" under their breath.

"Hey! Where's the patient that was in this room?" they heard a male voice ask with urgency.

"It's almost here. Just wait it out," Roman said, grasping Mina's shoulder. They could see the elevator on the second floor.

"She was being transported," a female voice said. "I've got the paperwork right here."

"Show me," came the angry voice before they heard him speaking into the radio every agent wore when protecting a witness.

The elevator dinged, and they pushed the gurney on. As soon as the doors slid shut, Roman cussed. "They're going to block the exits now. We have no way out."

"There's always the morgue," Marlise said with her eyes still closed. "Put the sheet over my face and take me to the sublevel. Have the ambulance back up to the loading dock."

Mina nodded at Roman, and he pulled his phone

from his pocket. While he filled in Mack, she leaned over and took the sheet, placing it over Marlise's face. "It won't be for long, I promise."

"I trust you, Mina," came her whisper from under the sheet.

The elevator dinged its arrival on the sublevel, and Roman slipped his gun under the gurney mattress as the doors opened. Mina knew he would shoot a threat first and ask questions later, so she prayed no one confronted them.

"Mack is pulling the ambulance up there now. We have to move before someone wonders why an ambulance is picking up a dead body," he whispered from behind his mask.

"Anyone watching the security camera would also wonder why we were running with a dead body."

"I know. Eyes on the prize. The Gruesome Two-some unites."

She bit back a snort and picked up a little speed with the gurney, hoping it looked like she was just anxious to get the body dropped off and get back to work. Of course, chances were good security had already been alerted to the missing patient, so if there were cameras down here, it would be obvious what they were doing.

They were almost to the doors of the morgue when they heard a commotion on the stairs. "Time's up!" Roman hissed, taking control of the gurney and pushing it through the doors. Mina followed, her boot thunking against the tile floor as they made a break for the bay where the coroner's van usually sat. Luckily for them, the coroner was out picking up a body.

Mack was waiting with the doors open and his butt planted firmly in the driver's seat. Roman pushed the gurney into the ambulance, followed it in and lifted Mina right off the dock and onto the bench seat in one motion. He grabbed the doors to close them while yelling, "Go!"

He got the doors secured and steadied the gurney when Mack hit the gas and squealed out of the hospital parking lot. "Your blood pumping yet?" Mack asked with a laugh as he spun them to the left. He flipped the emergency lights and siren on, hoping the cops coming at him wouldn't look twice as he went the opposite direction. They didn't, and he kept the lights and sirens going as he worked his way back to the airport over twenty miles away.

Roman lowered the gurney and made sure the wheels were secure in their moorings as Mina flicked the sheet off Marlise's face. "Piece of cake," she said, giving the scared and battered woman a wink. "We got you."

Marlise sat up when Roman loosened the straps and threw her arm around Mina. "I can't believe you're here! I've been so worried about you."

"I can say the same," Mina promised. "Listen, can you walk?"

Marlise nodded carefully but grimaced a bit with the motion. "They broke my arm and my nose, and my head hurts, but I can walk as long as you take this IV out."

Mina glanced up at the bag and made an executive decision. "I'm going to take it out now. We'll have to move quickly from the ambulance into the plane. Once we get back to the safe house, the nurse will put one back in if you need it."

Marlise rolled her eyes. "I don't need this one, but no one was listening to me. Just take it out."

Roman handed Mina the supplies, and she made fast work of getting the IV out. She was glad she'd been trained in basic medical procedures in the field. Now she needed to get this poor girl somewhere safe to talk. She tried to keep her head in the game, but seeing Marlise's face and arm kept sending her back to the night of the fire. Her friend had been badly burned, and while it had healed, the skin on her face and shoulder had finely webbed scars just like the ones covering her own foot. Marlise was injured on her watch, and shame filled her. She'd failed to do her job and—

"We're fifteen minutes out," Mack relayed, breaking into her thoughts. "Cal has the engine running."

"Who is that?" Marlise asked, her eyes wide as she took in the man driving the rig. He made Roman look small, so Mina could see why she'd be scared. "That's Mack."

"Another agent?" Marlise asked, and Mack let out a hearty guffaw from the front.

"Darling, I'm better than an agent. I'm untraceable."

Roman sat on the bench seat across from the stretcher. "Mack works for my brother, Cal. Not my brother by blood, but by life." Marlise nodded her understanding. "Cal is ex-military like me but prohelp when it comes to getting people out of sticky situations. We'll take care of you far better than the FBI did. I'm sorry for what happened yesterday."

"Hey," she said with a rueful smile, "I got some licks in." She held up her arm and turned the cast back and forth. "It's not often you break your hand and wrist punching someone in the head."

Min laughed just as Mack jerked the ambulance to the right, throwing them back against the wall.

"We got company!" he yelled, his erratic driving telling them it wasn't good company. The bullets that hit the rear of the ambulance seconds later were all the proof Mina needed.

"Get her down," Roman yelled while he fumbled for his gun under the gurney. Glock in hand, he busted out the small window in the door to return fire. Mina pulled Marlise down behind the small supply cabinet.

"Stay there! I have to help Roman!"

She pulled her gun and stayed low until Roman ran out of rounds, then she popped up and started firing, getting her first glance at the car that was after them. It was a Dodge Charger. Supercharged.

It was going to be impossible for this ambulance to outrun them.

"That's not the good guys!" Mina yelled just as a bullet hit centimeters below the window on the door. She leaned back for a moment then took aim as the car came alongside them.

She saw the snap of the tire before she heard the bullet fire, and she grinned when the driver veered across the road in a fight to get control of the now three-wheeled power beast. Mack hit the gas and drew them ahead, the airport coming into view.

"Driver's-side tire is gone!" she yelled as she ducked so Roman could return fire while she reloaded.

"They didn't call you Eagle Eye August for nothing!" Roman said as he popped up with his gun and unloaded it on the car. "Looks like a bulletproof windshield, but I got a hit on it!"

Mina tag-teamed him and took aim while Roman reloaded. He'd made a spider web out of the windshield, but she had a better plan. She pulled the trigger four times before she made a hit on the front passenger tire. The car, already hard to control, became a sail as it went off the road and into the ditch.

"Go, go, go!" Mina yelled, falling to the floor as a barrage of bullets hit the back of the ambulance.

"We're going to have one shot at ditching this and getting on that plane," Mack yelled over the sound of the bullets pinging off metal. "We have to get in the air before they catch up. You know they aren't alone.

If Cal's plane ends up bullet-ridden, he's going to be madder than when the Packers beat the Vikings."

Mina noticed even Marlise laughed at that one. Roman held watch out the back window for the guys in the car. "There's another car approaching to pick those guys up! Pedal to the metal, man!" Roman yelled to Mack.

Mack's laughter filled the entire ambulance. "Dude, I hit pedal to the metal ten miles ago!"

Min noticed Roman pull away from the window, and he gently lifted her off the floor and onto the gurney. His hand grasped her chin. "Are you okay?"

"I'm fine, Roman." She took his hand down from her face. "Help Marlise."

He lifted Marlise off the floor and back onto the gurney next to her and then knelt to address them. "As soon as those doors open, you run like hell to the plane. There's no time for pleasantries. Grab a seat and buckle up. Cal will be rolling while the door is closing."

Both women nodded, and Roman popped up to check the back window. "Still clear, Mack!"

"Arrival in under one minute," he yelled back.

Mina put her arm around Marlise to steady her as the ambulance took a left at a high rate of speed. Cal's plane came into view, the door opening as Mack raced toward it, jostling them about in the metal rig like popcorn.

"We're going to keep you safe," Mina promised

Marlise, but it was as much for herself as anyone. "When we stop, don't look back, just run."

Marlise's eyes were round and terrified, but she nodded just as Mack swore loudly from the front.

"Incoming!" he yelled as his windshield cracked. "Let's keep them in the front. We're going out the back!"

He slid the ambulance to the left and hit it into reverse, driving backward as the car came at them from the other side of the airport. As soon as the ambulance rocked into a hard stop, Roman threw the doors open and jumped out. He immediately lifted the women down and sent them running.

"Mack!" Roman yelled just as the front door of the ambulance flew open. Leaving it open, he used it for cover while he ran for the back of the old cargo plane.

"Go! Go! Go!" Mack hollered, a bullet whizzing past Roman's arm as he headed for the plane. He glanced back at Mack, who was motioning for him to go, so he did, helping Mina and Marlise onto the cargo door and into seats.

The first time Mina saw the plane, she was nervous. It looked like it had been shot down several times and there was no way it would stay in the air. Then she saw the interior. It was state-of-the-art. Cal said he didn't see much point in putting lipstick on this pig when it always ended up with new bullet holes anyway. One thing was for sure, this old girl could easily handle the pathetic guns The Madame's team was using against her.

Roman jumped into the copilot seat. "Go!" He was motioning for Cal to roll just as a bullet hit the front windshield.

"Where's Mack?" Cal asked, pushing the throttle forward. "These guys better get out of my way, or I'm running them over!"

"Securing the doors," Roman answered. "Ladies, buckle up! We might hit a speed bump or two."

Mina helped Marlise fasten the shoulder harness since her arm was in a cast and then did the same for herself. She took Marlise's hand and let her rest her head on her shoulder. "We got you," she promised, her gaze meeting Roman's. Her breath hitched, and she pointed at his arm. "You're bleeding, Roman."

He glanced down at his left arm and noticed the blood, and Mina was already digging through the first aid kit for a roll of gauze.

"It's just a flesh wound. I felt the bullet whiz past me, but it must have caught my sleeve."

Mina wrapped his arm up with the gauze and slapped his right hand over it. "Keep pressure on it until we land."

"Not to worry," Cal promised, pulling back on the yoke as the old bird lifted into the sky. "Selina will patch him up, and then you can play nurse for the rest of the night."

His laughter filled the plane, but Mina and Roman weren't laughing. Mina was trying not to have a coronary knowing that Roman got hurt because of her demands. He was better off without her in his life, and as much as it killed her to admit that, when this was over, she'd have to leave Roman behind for good. His kiss from last night flashed through her mind, and she forced back a whimper. That was going to be easier said than done.

Chapter Twelve

Roman was not dealing well with the events of the day. While Mina was in the shower, he paced the room, clenching and unclenching his fists. Finally, he grabbed a bottle of Jim Beam and poured himself a shot. He hit that one back and lowered the glass to the table. That was too close for comfort. His heart hadn't stopped pounding since the firefight in the ambulance. Why? He knew if The Madame's men locked onto them at the airport, it wouldn't be long before they found them here. He had no other option, though. They had to stay here to get the answers necessary to put The Madame behind bars.

Cal had assured him that his men would stop any siege on the compound, and Roman knew he should trust him, but risking Mina's life repeatedly was becoming more difficult with every passing hour. It was his lack of action that put her in danger in Red Rye, and he couldn't let her keep risking her life. Yes, she was an FBI agent, but she was injured and there was no way she could outrun an attacker on that foot. He had to make a choice, so he made it.

Locating The Madame was their objective. It had been that way for twenty-six months, and he didn't want to make it twenty-seven. Mina would find her, and then together they'd take The Madame down.

The door to the bathroom opened, and Min came out, her hair in curls around her shoulders and her face pink from the warm water. She smelled of green apples, and he wanted her in his arms. In his bed. Roman wanted her no matter what, but he couldn't be selfish and tell her that yet. She was just starting to trust him again, and he had to give her time to know she could trust him in all aspects of life.

"Hi," she said, pointing at the bandage on his arm. "How is it?"

"It's fine," he promised with a wink. "I've gotten worse injuries at the gym. If you hadn't pointed it out, I wouldn't have even noticed."

"How are Mack and Marlise?"

Mack had taken a bullet to the shoulder on his way out of the ambulance. That was one more thing Roman regretted about agreeing to the mission.

"He's been stitched up. It was a through and through, and thankfully, it didn't damage anything important. He's already back on patrol. Marlise is resting comfortably from what Selina told me."

Mina noticed the glass on the table, filled it and took a shot herself. When she finished, she grabbed a second glass and poured two more shots. "To a successful mission," she said after she handed him one.

Roman clinked glasses with her and drank the

shot, but he didn't feel any pride in what they'd done. He'd barely kept them alive, and that wasn't something to brag about, in his opinion. "Hard to call that one successful."

"We got the girl," she said sharply. "That was our only objective. Tomorrow, I'll talk with her, and with any luck, her answers will open my eyes to what I can't see right now."

She walked to the bed, and Roman noticed she was wearing the boot rather than her brace.

"Did you hurt your foot?" He knelt and opened the Velcro to check, but she stopped him.

"It's okay, Roman. The boot lets me move faster than my brace does. Right now, in our situation, I thought it wise to keep wearing it until the risks have been mitigated."

Roman grabbed the tube of gel out of the drawer and loosened the straps. He tenderly lifted her foot from the boot and removed her sock. Gently, he massaged the gel into her skin. "Does it hurt less in the boot?"

"No, but I can go longer before it steals my breath away. I know it's beyond help now, but I can't worry about what will happen to it when this is over. Right now, I have to focus on protecting Marlise."

"Cal will protect Marlise."

"I mean in the future, Roman. If I can't figure out who's behind this operation in Red Rye, all of us will be dead by Christmas."

"Don't say that." Roman spit the words out

through clenched teeth. The thought of her dying on his watch was too much for him tonight. "You have the skills to locate her. It's only a matter of time until you find a thread that unravels the whole case."

"I may already have," she said as he lifted her leg onto the bed and propped a pillow under the foot, offering her some comfort for the first time all day.

Roman finished washing his hands and then joined her, sitting on the opposite bed. Sitting next to her, or worse, lying beside her, would result in consuming her from head to toe.

"Why didn't you say anything? What did you find?"

"I had just discovered it when you and Cal came down to discuss the mission. Once we got back, and Marlise was in too much pain to talk, I investigated it more. On the surface, the connection looks innocent, but I'm not sure it is."

Roman made the out-with-it motion. "What are you talking about?"

"Liam Albrecht communicates with a senator in Maine, Greg Weiss. I don't mean once or twice, either. I mean regularly."

Roman leaned in closer. "What kind of communication?"

"I hacked Liam's email account. The emails appear innocuous, but I can't be sure until I have more time to study them."

"They could just be friends."

"Could be," she agreed with a shrug, "but I can't

find any connection between them. They didn't go to school together or grow up in the same area. We know that someone with power has to be making these girls' pasts disappear."

"Does a senator have that kind of pull?"

"As a senator, he would have those resources at his disposal."

"We've had eyes on Marlise for a year. We still can't find who she was before she came to Red Rye. We don't even have a last name for her."

"None of the girls in the house had a last name, Roman. Marlise refused to tell you what her name was before she hooked up with The Madame?"

"Marlise was too terrified to speak to anyone but you."

Mina rubbed her forehead and then ran her hands down her face. "I cannot tell you how relieved I was to see her today. Until the bullets started flying and terror filled my gut."

"I think I know that terror better than anyone," Roman ground out, his hands clenching and un-clenching. "I was afraid I was going to lose you again when I'd just found you."

"I'm still an FBI agent, Roman." She used her partner voice to remind him, but he heard the waver of it. She wasn't convinced her words were true any more than he was.

"I know, but that doesn't mean I wasn't terrified."

"I get it. Every time you popped up to shoot, I wanted to pull you back down. I'm glad we refused

Cal's request to have a team of guys following the ambulance. We barely made it back to the plane. They never would have. This is so messed up," she sighed, leaning her head back on the pillow. "I have the city manager of a tiny one-horse town intercepting my messages. I have a senator from a state halfway across the country communicating with him. I have girls who can't be identified and one who was beaten within an inch of her life yesterday. Did I miss anything?"

"You missed the *we* in there. *We* have all those things. You aren't alone in this, Mina."

"I know, Roman. I've been alone for the last year, and I forget that I'm not anymore. It's no disrespect to you or Cal. I'm just frustrated because nothing makes any sense on the surface. There has to be something I'm missing, and I pray that Marlise has that piece."

"All we can do is keep digging. We already know someone in Red Rye City Hall blocked your message from getting to me. That means, if someone didn't use their IP address as a cover, they had access to that app."

"Which makes zero percent sense because no one had access to it except the people in the house. Me, The Miss, and probably The Madame wherever her throne sits."

"Wait, what?" Roman asked, standing up and walking over to her bed. "How much access did they have? You said the app wasn't hackable, and no one could see the information we kept in the cloud or the SOS button."

"Which is still true," she assured him quickly. "Other than those parts, which aren't even visible to them, I had to make The Miss and The Madame administrators. The app was written for them to use, so there was no way I could avoid that, which is why I coded the other parts separately. Administratively speaking, they can pause messages from going out of the app. I didn't use the SOS button with the first message. I used the regular app. I thought I would be on my way to you. I didn't expect to get jumped before I got out the door."

"Which is why the second message came through to my phone," he said slowly.

"Because I used the SOS button rather than a message."

"And you didn't do that the first time because?" he asked, his hands squeezing his knees to keep from shaking the woman in front of him.

"The SOS meant rescue with any means necessary. I was afraid if everyone came blaring in with guns, we'd take innocent lives, and the ones we wanted would get away. I didn't have a lot of time to weigh my options, Roman. I was told The Miss was out of the house, so I sent the message and planned to slip out the back door, rendezvous with you and then head back in protected by the team once I knew The Miss was there."

Roman took a deep breath and forced his anger

down. She was right. She couldn't have known that plan wasn't going to work, especially if she'd been given false information. If he'd been in her shoes, he probably would have done the same thing. He couldn't fault her for wanting to save lives.

"I can see what your train of thought was now. But how would Liam stop the message if he didn't have access to the app?"

"I honestly don't know. I'm going to dig into it more tomorrow. The Miss could have used the IP address of city hall to throw suspicion on them. I may never know for sure, but with any luck, Marlise can fill in some of these blanks. I hope she's doing okay."

When they'd arrived back at Secure One an hour after they left St. Paul, Marlise was crumbling. She was due for pain medication for her arm, and the adrenaline had worn off halfway through the flight, sapping her strength. Cal had carried her straight to the nurse without a word to anyone. Roman knew his brother called the shots here, so there would be no talking to Marlise until morning.

"I checked with Cal while you were showering. She's resting after the nurse gave her some pain meds and she had something to eat and drink. The nurse said she's stable and just needs time to heal. We'll get together in the morning once you've both had a night of sleep." Roman rubbed his face, the fatigue setting in now that his adrenaline had drained away. "Time for bed. Do you need anything?" he asked, pulling the covers over her before he switched off the light.

"You," she answered, grabbing his hand before he could go back to his bed.

"Mina," he said, but she tightened her hand around his. "I'm already struggling to keep my lips off yours. Sleeping next to you is out of the question. There are things I want to do, and they aren't appropriate for where we are right now."

Her gaze hooded. "Where we are right now? Do you mean the physical place or the emotional?"

"We're safe here physically. Emotionally is another story, Min. If I take you in my arms the way I've always wanted to do…" He shook his head rather than finish.

"It's been seven years," she said, her gaze holding his. "Don't you think it's time we stop pretending that we don't want each other? That we don't care about each other as more than partners?"

Roman set his jaw and sucked air in through his nose. "Min, admitting that I care about you as more than a partner isn't the hard part. The hard part is having you for a few brief moments in time and then losing you again. I can't go back to that feeling in my chest that I carried around for a year."

"Wow, I didn't see that coming."

"See what coming?" he asked harshly. "The truth?"

"Yeah, the truth. And the truth is, you're a coward. I thought I knew just about everything there was to know about you, but I was wro—"

He reacted before he thought. He had his lips on hers and his body plastered along the length of her before she could finish. She met him with the same level of passion and desire, pulling at his lips and pressing at his groin. Her soft moan was too much for him, and he stripped her of the skimpy pajamas she wore. Her warm skin dragged a moan from his lips. He stripped his shirt off, barely breaking the kiss long enough to do so, and then was back to filling his head with the taste of her. She was everything he'd dreamed her to be and more.

"Protection," he murmured against her lips. "I don't have any."

"We're covered," she promised, running her nails up and down his back to draw a shudder from him. "Just don't stop."

"Oh, baby. I couldn't if I tried," Roman moaned, his heart filled with the beauty of her. He wanted to be everything for her at a time when she had nothing.

She lowered his boxers slowly, sending a shiver down his spine. "I've wanted you for so many years, Roman," she whispered as he held himself back from taking her fiercely and with seven years of pent-up desire.

Roman kissed his way down her tender neck to the swell of her breasts, then raised his head to gaze into her eyes while he entered her. "Oh, sweet, Mina," he sighed on a gentle thrust. "My dreams couldn't hold a candle to this. To you. To us, together."

She lifted her head until her lips met his, and her moan filled his heart with a sensation that could only be one thing. Her cries of pleasure tore away at his control until he was primed to fire. He possessed her body the same way she possessed his heart, and when she shot off into the universe on a cry of ecstasy, she cemented herself inside his soul forever.

Chapter Thirteen

They walked down a long hallway to the med bay where Marlise had spent the night. Mina was tired, but she should have expected that when she'd spent three-quarters of the night loving the man walking next to her. Her chest had never felt this light and this heavy at the same time. She wanted him, and he wanted her, but their jobs made that complicated. She knew once they were back in the real world, he'd come to his senses about being with someone like her.

Maybe he already had. When they got up this morning, he went directly to the shower and shut the door. When he came back out, he kept the door shut to his thoughts and feelings about what had happened between them. He spoke as few words as necessary to her this morning, and Mina felt the space he was trying to put between them for what it was. Fear. She understood it even if she didn't like it or feel it. They were partners, and she didn't realize how much pain her yearlong disappearance had caused him until last night when they'd made love. Could she call it that? Could you call it *love* if both people weren't feeling that emotion?

Yes.

Unrequited love was real, but to be honest, she didn't feel it was unrequited. Roman had been as emotionally invested last night as she had been. He'd taken as much pleasure in her release as he had in his own. Whatever Roman was feeling this morning, she didn't think it was regret. It was fear reminding him of all the things that could happen to her if he let his guard down. She would have to be patient and let him reach his own conclusions about who they could be together. She already knew the answer. He'd given it to her last night when their bodies connected.

"You're quiet," Roman said as they neared the med bay.

"So are you," she responded in kind.

He stopped and grasped her shoulders, turning her to him. "My silence has nothing to do with regrets about last night."

"Mine either."

His nod was comforting, and it told her she wasn't wrong to feel this way. When he leaned down and gently kissed her, it soothed the burning in her soul. "I'm trying to separate Roman the man from Roman the agent. It's not easy, but I know it's necessary if we want to find The Madame. I can hold you when we're alone in our room, but everywhere else, I can't distract you from the objective. We have a job to finish as The Gruesome Twosome."

"No, Roman." She let out a sigh filled with the sadness that she kept buried inside her about her injury. "The Gruesome Twosome ceased to exist the moment I lost function in my foot."

He put his finger over her lips and dipped his brow. "You are still Special Agent August in my eyes. Act like it. Stop telling me you can't and step up. Do your job."

She pushed him away and grunted. "It's that easy, huh? Just forget about all the things you can't do and focus on the things you can do! Well, thank you, Dr. Phil!"

He stood there, arms crossed and his brows up in the air after she finished her tirade.

"Focus on the things you can do," Mina whispered. "Yes. Focus on the things you can do! How far is the med bay?"

Roman motioned down the hallway, and she half skipped, half jumped down the hallway to the door where Roman had to put in a code after scanning his thumbprint.

"High tech," she said with appreciation. "Cal is either incredibly paranoid or incredibly dangerous."

"Both," Roman answered as the door clicked and he pushed it open.

She walked through the door and found Marlise sitting on the bed, nursing a cup of coffee. "Hi," she said, sitting down next to her. "How did you sleep?"

"Like a rock, but I still feel a little hungover. Selina promises it's the concussion, and it'll improve."

Selina winked at them from across the room, where she sat at a desk. Mina admired the woman for working for Cal. She was a tiny little thing, barely five feet tall, but all fire. Selina wasn't afraid to stand up to anyone who wanted something not in the best interest of her patient. Mina had been comforted knowing Marlise was getting excellent care last night, even if she was frustrated that she couldn't talk to her immediately.

"I know you're recovering, so if you need to rest, just tell me, okay?"

"I'll be fine," Marlise promised. "I want to get this over with as much as you do. I'm tired of being shadowed by guys I don't know or even particularly like. Where does the FBI find these knuckle draggers?"

Roman bit back a snort before he answered her. "You mean the highly trained FBI agents assigned to your protection detail until Mina could be found?"

Marlise rolled her eyes at Mina. "Highly trained might be a stretch. The last one didn't do so hot." She lifted her arm before she lowered it to her lap again. "I shouldn't say too much. He did manage to save me before the guys finished me off. It would have been fitting if they had, I suppose. Considering my life so far, no one would miss me."

"This doesn't have to be the end of your story, Marlise," Mina said with compassion. "When we were living in Red Rye, we talked about what you thought your future looked like, but that all changed when you escaped The Madame's hooks."

"Have I, though?" she asked, her gaze on her arm. "From where I'm sitting, I would say she still has them firmly buried in me."

"That's fair," Mina agreed. "Let's find a way to stop The Madame together, so we can both have our lives back."

"Okay," Marlise said, finishing her coffee. "Where do we start?"

Mina grabbed her writing pad and pen. "The night of the fire. Or rather the day of the fire. All I remember is you telling me to run because they knew who I was. You called me by my real name. How did you learn I was an agent?"

"I overheard The Miss on the phone. She didn't know I was outside the door, but what I heard her say froze me in my tracks. She said we'd been infiltrated. Then she said one of the guards saw Junior Miss— and I knew that's what your nickname was in the house—with a guy the night before. They somehow figured out you were a special agent."

The guards were women in the house who accompanied the new girls on their first dates. Under the illusion they were being protected from violence, the truth was something else entirely. The guards were there to make sure they didn't steal from The Madame. Mina didn't have proof, but she suspected any girls who stole from The Madame would end up dead in a river. The house in Red Rye had been new enough that girls weren't turning over, but Mina suspected it would have only been a matter of time had it stayed open.

Mina glanced back at Roman, who was grimacing. "Hey," she said, grabbing his wrist. "We met once a week for months. If a guard followed me, it was because The Miss already suspected I wasn't who I said I was. This isn't your fault." She waited for his head nod before she turned back to Marlise.

"What happened next?"

"I went to the kitchen so I didn't get caught by one of the guards. I hoped you'd be back soon, so I could warn you. I didn't know they'd act so quickly to get rid of you."

"That's okay," Mina said, gently rubbing the girl's back. "You're doing great. Don't focus on what happened that night. Focus on the whole picture. You told me something a few days before the fire, which was why I had to meet with Roman. I can't remember what it was."

"You didn't tell Roman?" she asked with surprise.

"No," Roman said, his arms crossed over his chest. "She just said she was working on something and would know soon. She said she had to protect you. That's why the FBI questioned you so extensively."

Marlise glanced down at her lap, and for the first time, Mina noticed the shame she wore like a cloak. "I didn't want to talk to those men."

Mina glanced up at Roman while rubbing Marlise's back. He gave her a pained grimace, and she nodded her agreement. "I understand," she assured the woman. "I remember how scared you were in the Red Rye house. You were always afraid the next guy you had to go out with would be the one to hurt you."

Her head still hung when she spoke. "That's why I ingratiated myself as the cook. I was more valuable to them cleaning and running the kitchen than I was working jobs. Men, they didn't want me. They said I was too skinny, shy and dumb."

Anger filled Mina, but she kept her hand on Marlise's back. "Those men were wrong. You were the sharpest girl in that house. You saw everything, processed it all quickly and learned how to protect yourself. Don't ever let those scumbags make you feel bad about yourself. They couldn't land a girl like you if they tried, and that was the reason they had to pay for dates."

Marlise lifted her head and shook it. "I don't think so," she whispered. "The other girls told me there wasn't much dating going on. They were picked up, taken to dinner, occasional sexual favors were performed, and then money was exchanged. The money came back to The Miss, and the girls didn't get their cut for weeks."

Mina turned to Roman and lifted a brow. His expression told her he understood what was going on too. "When I booked the dates, I had the fee schedule. The law was such that they could not pay for sex. They were only paying for companionship or a date to a wedding or event."

Marlise nearly sucked her tongue down her throat trying not to laugh. "Sure, and if you believe that, I've got a bridge to sell you in Brooklyn."

"You're saying there was prostitution going on?" Mina asked. "None of the girls ever indicated that in the entire year I was there. I dug hard for the information too, but none of them would admit it."

"They knew better. If the girls slept with the men, they got a bonus from The Miss, but it could never be discussed. There were a few who did before you took the job, and they mysteriously disappeared."

Mina's heart pounded in her chest with that information. Girls had disappeared from the house in Red Rye before she'd arrived. If they could somehow tie any of the victims from the river drownings back to the house in Red Rye, they could put The Miss and The Madame away for life. They just needed the evidence. Unfortunately, it wasn't as if Mina could just roll into the FBI files and get the pictures of the girls they'd found in the river. She would have to let her team find the link once they had The Madame in custody. Her team. She had to stop saying that. She wouldn't be part of the team once they made it back to Minneapolis. Capturing The Madame would have to be the final feather in the cap of her FBI career.

"Did you ever sleep with any of these men, Marlise?"

"No!" she exclaimed, jumping backward and nearly falling to the floor. She was caught by strong, tatted arms and set back on the bed.

Mina was surprised to see Cal in the room. She was concentrating on Marlise and hadn't noticed him come in. That spoke volumes about his ability to be a ghost. Cal knelt in front of Marlise and murmured to her. He encouraged her to take deep breaths while Mina got up and walked over to stand beside Roman, shoulder to shoulder.

"I'm not surprised by the prostitution aspect," he whispered. "It was a given that it was going on."

"I suspected but couldn't prove it. It was a high-end call girl service that brought in big bucks. I wasn't in charge of the money, though. The Miss had control of that. You and I talked about how much money I could see coming into the house throughout the investigation. I wonder how much came in that I didn't know about."

"If I had to guess, I'd say millions. We may be dealing with an escort service to cover a money-laundering operation."

"Bring it in, clean it and send it back out. We need the who and the why."

Roman motioned at Marlise with his chin. "See if she knows anything else."

Mina sat beside Marlise again, and Cal moved off to the side, but Mina raised a brow at his protective stance over the tiny woman. She would have to ask Roman about that later. "Marlise, when you went on dates, did the men give you exactly how much the fee schedule said they owed?"

"Oh, no," she said, shaking her head. "They just

gave you a bundle of money and sent you on your way. At least they did with me. When I went on a date, they didn't even want to finish dinner. They just gave me the money and told me to go home. They said their plans had changed."

"And you brought the money back to The Miss. Did you count it first?"

Marlise shrugged. "I didn't need to count it. It was always in straps of one-hundred-dollar bills. Sometimes I got one strap. Sometimes there were more. It was never more than I could carry in my purse, though."

"A strap of hundreds is ten grand. That's far more than the agreed upon fee." From what Marlise was telling her, it sounded like money laundering at its finest. The next question might be tricky for Marlise to answer, but she asked it anyway. "Did the men ever give you or the other girls anything else?"

She shrugged but didn't answer. She just stared at the floor with her hair down over her face. Cal knelt again and tipped her chin up to meet his gaze. "We can't help you if we can't find these guys, Marlise. If you tell us everything you know, we'll make them pay."

Marlise sat holding Cal's gaze for a long time. Longer than Mina was comfortable with, but Cal didn't back down. He helped her find the place she needed to be in before she answered.

"The girls," she said, still staring at Cal, "sometimes they brought back drugs." Her words were whispered as though she were afraid they would hear her. "I know they were drugs because where I used to live there were a lot of them."

"Do you know what kind of drugs and how much?" Mina asked, finally pulling Marlise's attention away from Cal.

"They didn't play with the small stuff. It was hard drugs, and I worried most of it was laced. The drugs went to The Miss, too, but we weren't supposed to know about it. Only certain girls went on those dates."

"Ha!" Mina suddenly exclaimed. "That explains why Charlotte, Emilia and Bethany were so busy."

Marlise nodded her head in agreement. "They were the only ones who went on those dates," she said, putting dates in quotation marks. "I'm not supposed to know about the drugs." The tone of her voice went so low they all had to lean in to hear her. "I overheard Charlotte talking to The Miss once while I was cleaning. After I learned that, I started paying attention to when they went out on their dates." Her eyes shifted around the room before they settled on her arm. "I documented it, and I was going to give you the information, but everything happened so fast I couldn't. Then they trapped me in the house with the fire. I tried to get out of the house, but that's the last thing I remember before I woke up in the hospital."

A shiver ran through her, and Cal lowered his hand to her shoulder. "Don't think about the fire.

Remember what we talked about before—tunnel vision. The Miss is at the end of the tunnel. That's what you concentrate on."

Marlise sucked in a deep breath and then let it back out. "They used the dresses."

"The dresses?" Roman asked.

Mina turned to him. "Those three girls always took a change of outfit on their dates. I was booking them for large functions and events, often in a different state. They took a bag and a second dress with them."

"They sewed pockets inside the lining of the dress," Marlise said. "No one would suspect the dresses."

"Do you know who The Madame is? Or, for that matter, who The Miss is?" Roman asked the woman, who was looking paler with every passing minute. "The FBI could not find her anywhere in a database. None of the girls in the house were ever found in the system, including you. It was like you were just sent here as a fully grown adult."

"They were all like me," she whispered. "When they bought me, they changed my name. I think the same thing happened to the other girls."

"Bought you?" Roman asked, taking a step forward, but backing off when Mina held her hand out to him.

"Marlise, are you saying that The Madame forced you to come work for her?"

The young woman nodded her head but then

shook it, leaving her confusion evident in the room. Cal still had his hand on her shoulder and knelt before offering her a smile. "You can do this, and as soon as you're done answering their questions, you can rest."

"My real name is Mary, but they changed it to Marlise and made me learn an entirely new history about myself. When I was twenty, I was homeless and living on the street in Phoenix. They looked for women like me, but they never took more than one girl from each city. They pretended to like you. They got to know you. They brought you gifts and paid for hotel rooms. I didn't know that's what they wanted until it was too late, I swear!" she exclaimed, her body quaking with fear. "Please don't arrest me!"

"Shh," Mina whispered, taking Marlise's uninjured hand. "You aren't in trouble. What happened to you is called grooming. The Madame wanted to gain your trust so you'd believe her when she said you would have a better life if you went with her. Is that what they told you?"

Marlise nodded, wiping away a tear with her shoulder. "I believed them at first."

"Who was them?" Roman asked. "The Miss?"

"No, I didn't meet The Miss until we got to the house. There were two women, and they said they worked for an agency. I was dumb. I believed them."

"No," Cal said, his hand firmly on Marlise's back. "You weren't dumb. You were in a situation you wanted out of, and you saw a way to do that. You didn't know they were trying to deceive you."

"That's true," Marlise said on a sigh. "I just knew I didn't want to spend another winter on the streets. I'm going to end up right back out there when this is over, though. I was only working at the women's home because the FBI put me there. I don't know what I'm going to do."

Marlise broke down into racking sobs, and no matter how much comfort Mina or Cal offered, she was inconsolable. Selina came over and gave her an injection, settling her back onto the bed and pushing everyone else away. Mina stood next to Roman with her thoughts spinning out of control. She had to remember what happened, or they were all going to die.

Chapter Fourteen

Mina's fingers moved across the keyboard with frightening accuracy. Her eyes trailed the information on the screen but never looked down at her fingers. Roman was jealous. He could barely hunt and peck his way through a case report. Mina, on the other hand, had magic fingers…in more ways than one. She was one of the best they had in the bureau for coding and hacking. But those hands in bed last night were magic, and Roman wished they were back there. She found his thread and started to unravel it bit by bit until he lost control of himself. He was praying they would do it all over again tonight. Looking at her now, though, he doubted that would happen. That was okay. They had a case to concentrate on, a woman to arrest and their decisions to defend before they could think about their personal lives.

Since they'd left Marlise to rest, watched over by Selina and Cal, Mina had been at the computer while Roman twiddled his thumbs. Okay, so he was doing something. He was running the information through on a different computer whenever she called something out to him.

"I wish I had access to the bureau's files right now," Roman grunted. Trying to use Cal's software to run names wasn't nearly as effective as using the FBI's programs.

"The bureau's programs couldn't find who those girls were either, Roman, but there has to be a trace somewhere of who they were."

"Not necessarily. It depends on who The Madame reveals herself to be. If this person has connections, they might be able to wash away any evidence that a person existed."

"Which is why Senator Greg Weiss is my next target."

Roman tipped his head back and forth. "That's a stretch, Mina. We can't find any connection to Liam and Greg other than those emails. Not to mention, Red Rye is Nowhere, USA."

"Exactly," she agreed. "Hiding in plain sight or, in this case, small-town utopia. Red Rye is within driving distance of Denver, Kansas City, Oklahoma City, Albuquerque and, hell, Texas as a whole. I know this because I booked the three girls who worked the big events in all those cities. They're running the drugs out of the cities and using the girls in Red Rye to clean the money and redistribute the drugs. We didn't have that many girls in our house, but if there were the same number of girls in other houses, the money would add up quickly."

"Only Marlise was in the Red Rye house when we got there the night of the fire. Since then, we haven't found a trace of any of the other girls. They didn't fly out using the names from the Red Rye house."

"They didn't have to!" Mina exclaimed, taking Roman by surprise. "They had a private plane they used to transport the girls for events in cities too far away to drive."

"Marlise didn't tell us that when we asked her."

"She wouldn't have necessarily known, and even if she knew, she wouldn't know what airfield they used. I only knew because I had to call the pilot and set up the flights each time. Here," she said, brushing him aside. She started typing on his keyboard, her bottom in his face, and he grabbed her hips, a moan filling the room at the thought of how easy it would be to take her right there the way he wanted to. "Down, boy," she scolded, glancing behind her with a cheeky grin. "We're working."

"All work and no play makes Mina a very boring girl."

She snorted to hold in her laughter, but Roman felt it in the shake of her hips. "Look," she stood and motioned to the screen. "This is the airfield where they kept the plane. We need to find the flight plan and see where they went."

"Do you think The Miss was dumb enough to use the private plane you knew about to get them out of there? Much less file a flight plan?"

"The Miss thought I was burning alive in that

fire, but she underestimated Roman Jacobs, and that was her mistake."

Roman stood and pulled her into him, his lips landing on her warm ones and teasing them into a tangle of tongues neither of them would soon forget. "She better hope I never get my hands on her," he whispered with his lips barely off hers.

"Let's find her, and then I'll give you three minutes in an interrogation room with a faulty CCTV."

Roman grinned and kissed her again. "What do you think this is, television? No way that trick would work anymore. Besides, I'd never hit a woman."

He felt the grin on her lips as she kissed him one last time and stepped back.

"You're right, though. The Miss probably didn't file a flight plan. I would suggest we hack the airport's security cameras, but it's been over a year. There's no way they still have footage." She ran her hands through her hair. "I just want to go home."

Roman wanted to take Mina to his home and never let her leave. First, they had to put this case to bed, but they were no closer now than a year ago. "The FBI has run continual facial recognition on every major airport in the country looking for her, but I've known that was futile. If she did fly into a major city, she'd wear a disguise."

"I wish I knew if they took the plane that night. There is no way to know, though."

"What about the pilot? You said you had contact with him."

"I did," she confirmed, her hands flying over the keyboard again, "but I only had his first name. Probably not his real one either, so that's a dead end too."

She fell silent for ten minutes as she typed away, all her attention back on the screen in front of her. Roman was going through flight plans over the last year on the off chance he'd get lucky when the clacking stopped, and she leaned forward.

"Roman," she said, a tremor in her voice. "Do city managers have campaign funds?"

"Usually, a city manager is appointed by the mayor. Only the mayor would need a campaign fund. Why?"

She pointed at the screen. "I finally got into Liam Albrecht's bank statements. For two years, he was making large cash donations to a campaign fund."

"How large?" Roman asked, walking over to stand behind her as she pointed at the screen.

"Between eight and nine grand every week, but never more than nine grand."

"Ahh, yes. Money laundering at its finest," Roman said, his hands on his hips. "Was the campaign fund his?"

"I haven't gotten that far," she said, putting her hands back on the keyboard. "But there's no way a city manager can afford to donate almost forty thousand dollars a month to someone's campaign. That doesn't make sense."

"It does if he's The Madame," Roman said slowly.

Mina spun toward him. "No way. We pulled three

times that much money into the house on a bad day, Roman. Just in cash. That's not including the drugs."

"Has to be a cartel. The fund was probably just a front for a cartel. A way to wash the money a few times before it got back to them."

"Could be," she agreed. "The deposits stopped the same week the house in Red Rye burned."

"Convenient," Roman said with his brow in the air. "Can you see if that account is closed?"

Roman knelt next to Mina, patiently waiting while she typed away as if her life depended on it. Then again, it did. If she didn't find The Madame, she'd always be a target. He knew his Mina, though. She'd already found a thread, and she was starting to unravel it.

In ten minutes, she hit the keyboard a final time and waited while information filled the screen. "Look, the account was closed, and the money was transferred to two separate accounts, both of which are campaign fund accounts."

"Which means they know they can't use offshore banking anymore."

She nodded. "At least not for very long. The new regulations require banks to report every quarter, and that's going to send up a red flag if large amounts of cash are dumped in and then pulled out every few months."

Roman paced the small space as she went back to typing. He was waiting for answers, and there was little he could do other than be the muscle for her at this point. She held the power in her hands to solve this case, not him.

"Well, well," she said somewhat sarcastically, and Roman was next to her in an instant. "Looks like The Madame found a new home." She pointed to the screen with an account number and almost a year's worth of the same kind of deposits. "This account belongs to…" she typed some more until she tipped her head to the side. "The mayor of Santa Macko."

"Where the hell is that?" Roman asked over her shoulder.

"Near the border of California and Arizona."

"Well, a mayor would need a campaign fund."

"Do me a favor," she said, but Roman could hear she was distracted and trying to work the problem. "Run Santa Macko through Cal's program. Get me population and how long the mayor has been there."

Roman went to his desk and sat down, entering the terms into the computer. She was already back to typing while he waited for the information to come up on his screen. When it did, he was more than a little surprised. "The population of Santa Macko is under two thousand people. The mayor was elected in an uncontested election two years ago. Benjamin Bartos. He's forty-three and moved to Santa Macko three years ago."

"Just in time to get his residency in place for the mayor's race."

"You think he's a plant?"

"I don't think a mayor who ran uncontested needs a campaign fund of half a million dollars."

She rubbed her hands over her face and sighed. "This whole thing is weird. The Madame's business is still active since they're depositing money, but it was easy to follow the money from Liam to Benjamin, which is also weird. I will have to hack into the housing records for Santa Macko and look at purchase or rental dates for all the properties in the area. It'll be the only way to know if The Madame set up shop to start laundering again."

Roman stood and walked to her, gently rubbing her shoulders. "Not tonight, though."

"Yes, Roman, I can't stop now. We're too close to The Madame to quit."

"Maybe," he insisted, turning her to him. "But even if we are, you're too exhausted. You'll need patience for that much hacking, and that means you need food and sleep first."

"Every day we wait is a day The Madame could slip away," she insisted, her shoulders stiff.

"Min, you know I'm right. There comes the point where your body needs rest. We've reached that point."

This time her shoulders slumped under his hands, and he knew he'd won this argument. At least for the time being. She stood and wrapped her arms around his waist, resting her head on his chest.

"I want this to be over for you and Marlise."

"And I want this to be over for you," Roman whispered, rubbing her back. "You didn't ask for this when you went undercover. You deserve to live your life."

"I kind of did, though," she muttered, and Roman could hear the fatigue of the last year in her words. "I agreed to the undercover operation knowing I was putting myself at risk. I was willing to take that risk to myself to save the girls at the house. All I did was make things worse. Marlise will never be the same, and the other girls are still with The Madame."

"The girls who are still with The Madame are there because they want to be. That's not on you."

"The Madame could still go after Marlise as a pawn."

"She could," Roman agreed, "but right now, the only person she wants is you."

Mina gasped and leaned back. "Then let's give her what she wants!"

Roman cocked his head. "What?"

"Think about it, Roman," Mina said, starting to pace but thinking better of it and resting her butt on the desk. "We know she wants me, so we should give her what she wants."

"No," Roman said as soon as he understood what she meant. "You are not going to be bait for a psychopath. Forget it. You can barely walk, much less protect yourself."

Her temper flared, and she stuck her finger in his chest. "I am not unable to protect myself. I managed for the last year, thank you very much! I don't need a man to push me behind his back and protect me!"

Roman smiled. There was the Min he used to know. She was still hiding in there, waiting to come out. Regardless, she wasn't going to be bait. "Forget it. I just found you. There is no way I'm going to agree to this."

"We may not have any other choice, Roman," she said. The dejection in her tone had him slinging his arm around her shoulder as they walked to the ladder.

"Maybe not, but right now, we still have options. If we don't get anywhere with those in the next few days, we can revisit the idea."

He helped her climb the ladder to their room and closed the door behind them. "For now, you need some downtime so you can look at things with a fresh perspective again."

Roman waited for her to balk and try to convince him to keep working, so he was surprised when she agreed. "You're right. I need a shower, food and medication. My foot is better in this boot, but it's on fire after being down so long."

"Can you shower alone, or do you need help?" Roman asked, grasping her arm to keep her upright.

She raised a brow and took a long perusal of his body. "Oh, I most definitely need help," she said, throwing him a wicked grin. She hooked her finger under his chin, turned and walked to the bathroom, Roman following right behind her just like he always would.

"WE SHOULDN'T BE *meeting like this out in the open*," Roman said, glancing around the woods they were standing in.

"We're not in the open," Mina said. "I had to see you. Listen, I don't have long, but something big is going down tomorrow at the house."

"What?" Roman asked, locked into the conversation now.

"I don't know for sure, but it may be that The Madame is finally going to show her face at the house."

"Not likely."

"Okay, maybe not her real face, but the vibe I got was a VIP will arrive at ten p.m. tomorrow. If it is The Madame, I'll somehow figure out a way to get prints."

"How do you know someone is coming in?" Roman asked while his trained eye flicked about the trees looking for threats.

"I overheard The Miss telling some of the guards to be ready for a personal car to arrive at ten p.m."

"Is there any way you can get the information sooner rather than later?"

"I don't see how since I'm not supposed to know. I do know this person is bringing three new girls for the house."

Roman's brow went up. "Did you lose girls?"

"Nope, but we have empty bedrooms, and they want them filled. More girls equal more money. Plus, Marlise isn't going out anymore. She's taken on the role of cook and housekeeper."

"I'm surprised The Miss allows that."

"Let's just say that Marlise is never requested a second time by any man. She's too meek and shy. Since she's willing to do the cooking, shopping and cleaning, The Miss sees it as a win. They don't have to bring anyone in from the outside, and it keeps Marlise from leaving the house to give away any secrets."

"I don't think she'd get very far if she tried," Roman muttered.

"She wouldn't make it to the county line before she disappeared. She knows it too. These girls are nobodies, and that's the way The Madame likes it. She can dangle carrots she knows they'll take just to stay alive."

"We need to get this woman, Mina. For all the girls in this house and any other ones. Have you made any progress on the locations of other homes?"

"Yes," she whispered, glancing around the darkening woods. "I know for sure there's one in Seattle, Billings, Atlanta, Dallas, Miami, Chicago, Philadelphia and Washington D.C. Those are just the ones I'm sure about."

"Do you have exact locations?"

"No, if I did, we'd already be out of this one-horse town. I let the powers that be know to look for houses in those cities, but you know that'll take a significant amount of time and manpower. We need to be patient until I can get more information to zero in on the addresses."

"Right, patience. I'm running low after a year of this back and forth. Also, why would they have houses in all those cities and stick one right in the middle of nowhere? That doesn't make sense."

"I know, I was thinking the same thing. If I had to guess, I would say it's because Red Rye is centrally located to the bigger cities. All I know is, they trust me now, and I'm hoping that's why I've been invited to be there. Be ready tomorrow night, Roman. Something big could go down, and I want the team in place. If we're lucky, we get The Madame tomorrow night, but if things go south, I'm going to need backup, and I'm going to need it fast."

"Get back to the house. I'll rally the team and be ready when you say the word."

Mina nodded and turned to go, but Roman grabbed her shirt and hauled her into him. "Promise you'll say the word before it's too late, Min."

"I promise," she whispered, her gaze locked with her partner's. If only he didn't have that cardinal rule, she'd lay her lips on his right that second. She wanted to, but she couldn't handle the sting of his rejection tonight and stay on her game with The Miss when she got back to the house.

"I won't lose you to them, Min. Do not play. If anything feels off, pull the rip cord. We have enough to shut them down already."

"We need The Madame, or at the very least, her real name. You got my back, Jacobs?"

"Just like I always do, and your front and sides,"

he promised. "Get this woman so we can go home. I'm tired of Nowhere, USA."

"You and me both, but I can't abandon these girls, Roman. They have no idea how much they're being used. They're trading their bodies for the stability they've never had. That's not fair. I won't walk away from them."

He pulled her into a quick hug before releasing her. "I know. That's what I love about you, Min. You never give up on the underdog. Get back to the house now. I'll get the team in place."

Mina woke with a start. *"That's what I love about you, Min."* How many times had the memory of that sentence gotten her through the long nights over the past year? Too many to count. He didn't even mean it in the true sense of the word, but it made her feel less alone to remember that there was a time when she had someone covering her back.

She flipped around and gazed at the man who was wrapped tightly against her while he slept. The lines of worry and fatigue were replaced with the abandonment of sleep. He was relaxed, and she loved the look on him. She rarely got to see Roman Jacobs relaxed, not only now but throughout their career. He took their job seriously, and he often took the job home with him. Some of that was her fault, but a lot of it was just who he was as a person. He didn't like doing a job halfway. It was all the way, or it was no way. That was the reason he hung in with her so long in Red Rye. He understood she couldn't leave those girls to the mercy of The Madame. She knew they weren't there against their will, but she quickly learned that they were willing to give up their autonomy to stay in the house and work for The Miss.

Mina could never understand why until she talked to Marlise. For most of those girls, the house in Red Rye represented something they'd never had before in their lives, even if that meant giving yourself to men you didn't know. Marlise was smart. Early on, she figured out those men didn't like shy, quiet girls who stumbled over their words and didn't make eye contact. She used her natural personality to her advantage. She found a way to stay in the house and keep the stability it offered, but managed to make herself invisible while doing it.

Mina slipped out of bed and strapped the boot on, limping to the hatch door and lifting it quietly. For the last year, all she remembered was the one sentence of that memory. Tonight, she had the whole picture. All she had to do was find one other house on the string, and she'd be able to break the code of The Madame's game. She'd work while Roman slept, and with any luck, by the time he woke up, she'd have the name for the face in her nightmares.

Chapter Fifteen

Mina cursed the pain in her foot for the ten millionth time as she stretched it out to the side of the computer desk. When she got out of this mess, she was going to have to see a doctor. Something told her what they had to say would not be positive. Mina knew there was no saving the foot, but she forced the thoughts of it from her mind and went back to searching for a connection between Red Rye and Santa Macko.

She hadn't said anything to Roman, but she was about seventy percent sure that Liam Albrecht and Benjamin Bartos knew each other. She also suspected that, somehow, they were both tied to Greg Weiss. Nothing else made sense. Not to mention, if someone at the city manager's office were on the payroll, they'd be more willing to convince the authorities not to ask too many questions about what went on at 798 South Hampton Road in Red Rye. That address was burned into Mina's mind forever. She hated that everything went sideways before she could shut down the whole operation. Those girls were still suffering because she couldn't get the job done. Mina didn't care about herself anymore, but she wasn't going to let girls like Marlise suffer any longer.

One glance at the clock told her two hours had passed since she'd started working. She was waiting for one more search to finish, and then she'd have to give it up for the night. It was nearly two o'clock, and if she didn't get more sleep, Roman would be after her tomorrow about resting.

Her screen froze, and she snapped her attention back to it, waiting to see if it was a glitch or a home run. A picture popped up on the screen that made her heart pound the way it always did when she got a pertinent piece of information on a case. This was a home run.

She needed to show this picture to Marlise, but there was no way to print anything. She couldn't leave it on the screen because she wasn't sure how long it would be before the search timed out. She was about to call Roman when the thought stopped her in her tracks. Call. She still had the phone Cal had given her when they went to get Marlise. She couldn't do much with it, but it did have a camera.

She pulled open every desk drawer until she found the phone. When she snapped it open, she was relieved to see it was still over half charged. She did her best to take a good picture of the computer screen and then tucked the phone in her pocket. She left the picture up on the screen in hopes it wouldn't disappear before she got back, but if it did, at least she had the image on the phone.

Once up the ladder, she closed the hatch quietly and walked to the bed. "Roman, are you awake?"

He grumbled in his sleep, but his eyes never opened. Mina needed to see Marlise now, even if that meant waking her up. If Mina was right, they'd found their thread, and she could finally unravel the mystery of The Madame and her game.

"Roman," she said, shaking his foot, but he snored on, his body relaxed in sleep. The shower they'd shared had probably added to his relaxation, she thought with a smirk. She had to give it to him. He wasn't afraid to love her now.

That's not what this is, Mina, she scolded herself. This is forced proximity mixed with fear. As soon as they were back in Minneapolis, there was no way he'd continue to sleep with her. Not once she addressed the situation with her foot. A man like Roman Jacobs would not start a relationship with a washed-up FBI agent who couldn't walk.

She sighed as she watched him sleep. The truth was painful, but it was the truth all the same. Regardless of what they had to do to her foot, she would no longer be an FBI agent, which meant they would no longer be partners. They both knew it.

The truth was, she didn't want to go back to the bureau. Her stint at Red Rye had taken a toll, and her undercover days were over. Her days of chasing suspects and bringing in the top-ten most-wanted criminals were also behind her. What wasn't behind her was The Madame, and she would see this one to the very end if it killed her. And it might. She would accept that if it meant she saved the other girls in the process.

She grabbed a sheet of paper off the counter and wrote a note before leaving it on the table and sneaking out the door of the room.

Chapter Sixteen

"Everything all right, special agent?" asked the guard, who stood to his full height with his hand on his radio.

"Yes, it's fine," Mina assured him. "I need to talk to Marlise. Will you walk me to the guest cottage she's in?"

"It's almost three a.m., ma'am," he said with his head cocked.

"I'm aware, and if you call me *ma'am* again, Eric, I'm going to show you how an FBI agent takes down a mercenary."

He stifled a snort but couldn't hide the grin. There was no way she was taking down his nearly three hundred pounds of muscle, but he didn't argue with her, which she appreciated. He pressed the button on his radio and spoke into it.

"Agent August is requesting a moment with the patient."

Mack's voice was loud and clear when it came across the radio. "Tell Agent August it can wait until morning. The patient is asleep, and Cal doesn't want her disturbed."

Mina raised her brow. Cal doesn't want her disturbed? Now he was calling the shots instead of Selina? She nodded for Eric to press the button again, only this time, she stepped up. "Consider her told and consider her not to care. Wake her up. We'll be there in ten minutes."

Eric released the button, and Mack responded with a heavy sigh and a ten-four. He knew he would get chewed out by Cal in the morning, but he'd do what she said anyway. After all, she was still the FBI.

Eric walked with her through the lodge and across the rutted grass, keeping his hand under her elbow to ensure she didn't fall. She seriously regretted not bringing the cane with her that was leaning up against the wall in their room. Cal had moved Marlise to the cabin at the back of the property to give her a view of the lake while she recovered, and although that was great for Marlise, it was destruction on Mina's sore foot.

"I'll wait outside with Mack," Eric said as they neared the small, one-bedroom cabin.

She noticed a light burning inside, which meant Mack had done what she'd asked and woken up Marlise.

"When you're done, I'll walk you back. Does Roman know where you are?"

"I left him a note," she explained. "He was sleeping, but this couldn't wait. If Marlise can verify my evidence, then I am one step closer to finding the person behind this."

"Be careful," Eric warned her, helping her up the steps to the cabin. "Those guys meant business the other day at the airport."

"They've meant business since I first ran into them in the house in Red Rye. They mangled my foot beyond repair for funsies, their word not mine, and then tried to kill me by leaving me to die of smoke inhalation. When that didn't work, they came after me in the woods like ninjas in the night. They probably would have succeeded that time if it hadn't been for Roman. Hey, Mack," she said, sliding the greeting in nonchalantly as though they'd been talking about the weather rather than the many ways she could have died in the last few years. "I'm sorry to bother Marlise, but this is important."

"Too important to wait until morning?"

"Technically, it is morning." Mina winked, and Mack groaned while he held the door open for her.

"Don't stay long. She's exhausted, and I'm already going to get my butt chewed out for allowing this."

"I'll take the heat, but this won't take long."

He closed the door behind her, and Mina walked to the bedroom. When she stuck her head inside the door, she wasn't surprised to see the young woman wide awake and sitting up in bed.

"Hey, Marlise. Sorry to wake you up."

"It's no problem. I wasn't asleep. I don't sleep well anyway, but my arm is sore. Selina is going to give me some medicine once we're done talking. Maybe then I can get some rest."

"I'm sorry you're still in pain, Marlise. That's on me. I'll carry that forever."

"Nonsense," she said with a shake of her head. "I was with The Madame long before you showed up. I sold my soul for a chance at a better life, and the soul reapers came calling. I won this time. That doesn't mean I'll win the next time. I'll help you any way I can."

"No," Mina said, gently hugging her friend. "You didn't sell your soul. You trusted people because you wanted out of a bad situation."

"Only to put myself in a worse one."

"But you didn't know that at the time. There was no way for you to leave once you were there, either. You know that, right?" Marlise nodded, but her gaze fell to the cast on her arm. Mina tipped her chin back up. "I know you don't believe me, and I wish I could have told you this when we lived at the house together, but let me say it now. You were the smartest one in the house. You played the game better than any of them because you learned how to protect yourself. You used your natural talents against them."

"You mean being shy and afraid of my shadow?" Her laughter held no mirth, and Mina squeezed her hand.

"Yes. If I hadn't had you there at the house with me watching my back, I'd be dead. You were so good at not being noticed that you blended in, and that earned you information I would never have gotten."

"I didn't do that on purpose," she said quickly, as though what she had done was wrong.

"I know you didn't, Marlise. I just meant that without even knowing it, you kept me alive. I need your help one more time, and then I can help you in return."

"I'll do anything," she promised, shifting in the bed. She appeared uncomfortable, and Mina wanted to get the information so she could rest.

"You were at the house about three months before I got there, correct?"

Her head shook instantly. "No, I was the first girl The Miss brought to the house, so it was closer to six months before you arrived. I guess she thought she saw something in me that wasn't there when push came to shove."

"What do you mean?"

"She couldn't shine me up like the other girls. I wasn't good at being confident and strutting around on heels. Forget about makeup."

"You're saying they worked with you at the house before they started the escort service?"

"Of course. The recruiters told us we were going to a home where we'd learn to be self-sufficient, take care of ourselves and get a job. I believed them, too. I was desperate to find a home. I was attacked three times on the street, and I was afraid the fourth time would kill me."

"I know you had it hard out there, Marlise. Even though Red Rye wasn't what they promised, you still felt safer?"

"I did at first," she said, "but then the men started coming to the house."

"You mean men came to the house before I got there?"

"In the beginning, yes. Supposedly, the men came so we could practice going on dates. However, more than innocent dating occurred, and I think the police found out."

"Why do you think that?"

"Well, the men stopped coming after The Miss had a cop knock on the door one day. I was standing there and heard her tell them the men were from the city, and they were just inspecting the house. She told the cop to talk to city hall about it. After that, we never saw another man in the house. Instead, we started going away on the weekends to practice our dates at hotels. No one asked questions there."

"I see," Mina said, trying to take in all the information and sort out what was important. Her mention of city hall had her brain spinning, but she didn't want to plant any ideas in Marlise's head before she showed her the picture. "If I show you a photo, can you tell me if you've ever seen the people in it before?"

"I can try," she said on a shrug.

"Don't worry about it if you don't recognize them, okay?" Mina smiled encouragingly while she pulled out her phone. She hoped the somewhat grainy image was enough to trigger recognition for Marlise. She held up the phone and was shocked when her friend's eyes closed, and she pushed the phone away.

"I'm not supposed to talk about them," she whispered. She trembled when she spoke, and Mina had to lean in to hear her.

"It's okay to talk to me, Marlise. If these people were involved with the Red Rye house, they might help me find The Madame. Isn't that what you want?"

"Yes," she whispered.

Before Mina could say anything more, Cal materialized in the room. "I said she wasn't to be disturbed."

Mina fought hard against the threatening eye roll. She wouldn't disrespect what he was doing here, even if it made it hard for her to get the information she needed.

"Cal, I know you've saved my bacon more times than I can count the last few days, and I am not trying to be ungrateful, but I have a lead. If I wanted to continue living my life and free Marlise to do the same, I needed to ask her a question."

"It couldn't keep until a saner time of the day?"

"No," she whispered, "because every hour that passes is another hour closer to The Madame finding us."

"I wasn't sleeping anyway," Marlise said, her

shoulders stiff. "My arm was bothering me. Mina is okay here."

Cal softened after the woman spoke. "Fine, but you need to rest, so wrap this up."

He stepped out into the hall, and Mina fought a smile as Marlise chuckled. "He's like a combination of a jailer and a bodyguard all wrapped up in one."

Mina was relieved to hear her friend laugh, so she joined in. "I would say he's used to people doing what he says without any pushback."

"I guess he isn't used to strong women then, is he?" Marlise asked, squaring her shoulders. "I'm going to tell you what I know about those men because I trust you. If anyone can get us out of this mess, it's you."

"And if I can't, I'm going to go down trying." Her promise was made with a squeeze of Marlise's hand.

Marlise picked up the phone again and pointed to the picture. "They both used to come around the house when we first got to Red Rye. We practiced our dates with them." Her words stuttered, and she cleared her throat before going on. "This one," she pointed to the man on the left, "he would go upstairs with some of the other girls. They said he was just helping them with private tutoring. I might not have gone to high school, but I'm not an idiot. I knew what was going on up there. I was just glad I didn't have to be part of it."

"This guy didn't do the same personal tutoring?" Mina asked, pointing to the man on the right.

"He only came to the house twice before he stopped coming with the other guy. I never saw him again once The Miss started taking us to hotels for the practice dates."

"Do you know their names?" Mina asked, tucking the phone back in her pocket.

"No, but I'm sure they aren't Tom and Jerry like they told us they were."

A heavy sigh escaped Mina's lips. No, they weren't Tom and Jerry. She knew who they were, but that didn't matter to Marlise tonight. "That's okay. Thanks for being honest with me about knowing them. I know who they are, and now I can tie them into finding The Miss and then The Madame. I'm going to go back to the house so you can get some rest. I'll have Cal send Selina in with some medication?"

"That would be great," she said, her head falling back to the pillow and exhaustion falling across her face like a blanket. "I would love to get some sleep."

Mina patted her shoulder. "I'll see you later."

She turned, but Marlise grabbed her sleeve. "Can you find her now?"

Mina's smile was forced, but she hoped the girl wouldn't notice. "Now that I know these two men were involved, I have a trail to follow. That's only because you were brave enough to tell me the truth. I need to work for a few hours, but I'll have Mack and Cal keep you informed when you wake up. I want you to rest."

"Okay. Good luck," she whispered, her eyes going closed. "I'll see you tomorrow."

Mina walked out, stopping next to Cal when she found him in the living room. "She's requesting some medication for her arm. It's keeping her awake. Do we need to take her back to a hospital?"

Cal stood to his formidable size and shook his head. "No. Selina said the first few days after a break like that would be rough. I'll take care of her. Did you get what you need?"

"Yes," she sighed. "I wish I hadn't had to wake her, but it was the fastest route to the answers I needed. I'm going back to the lodge. There's work to be done."

"Mack is waiting to escort you. Fair warning, Jacobs is madder than a wet hen that you didn't wake him. Be ready for a tongue lashing when you get back."

Her laughter filled the cabin as she walked to the door. "This is not my first rodeo with Roman Jacobs. I can handle him with one hand tied behind my back."

Cal grinned and tipped his head to the left. "Since you showed up, my bet has been on you all along."

Cal gave her a finger gun and then walked into the other room, leaving Mina to wonder what he meant by that. She shook it off and headed down the porch with Mack, the sky still eerily black as it neared four in the morning. Storm clouds had rolled in overnight, and her foot told her the storm was going to be a doozy.

"We're one step closer, Mack," she said to the man walking next to her, his hand grasping her elbow.

"I sure hope so because Roman is on his way over here now. He's spitting mad that none of us stopped you from leaving the room. We should probably double-time it back before he meets us halfway. You should not mess with a man in love."

"A man in love?" she asked, a brow raised in the air, even if it was too dark to see.

"Calling it as I see it," Mack said with a shoulder shrug. "When you two are together, it's pathetically easy to see you're in love. The way you make googly eyes at each other is enough to—"

"I get it, Mack," Mina said, forcing a chuckle, though it sounded as fake as it was. "We need to slow down. My foot can't handle the terrain this quickly."

They slowed, and suddenly, Mina was yanked backward with a hand over her mouth. Her arms were pulled behind her, and her feet left the ground. A hulking man dressed in all black was in hand-to-hand combat with Mack, but Mack wasn't winning. She had to help him! Mina kicked upward with her cast boot, trying to catch her assailant with the rubber sole. Before she could twist to fight back, a fist came at her. The last thing she saw was Mack dropping to the ground before the blackness closed in around her.

HIS GUT DIDN'T LIE, and right now, his gut said to find her. Roman jogged down the hallway to the back door and scanned his thumbprint, waiting impatiently for the system to recognize him and open the door. When it finally clicked, he squeezed through the slit before it had a chance to open all the way. He headed across the lawn for the cottage where Cal had moved Marlise earlier today. If Roman didn't know better, he'd think Cal had a crush on the woman. Roman knew better. His brother never dated. Cal preferred no-strings-attached kinds of relationships. Considering what they'd both seen of human nature over the years, Roman understood it. He wasn't much of a dater himself before seven years ago, when he met Mina August for the first time. Dating hadn't happened at all since then. Roman always blamed it on the job, but he knew that wasn't fair to the job.

The truth was, he knew it wasn't fair to compare every woman he took out to Mina, and that was precisely what he'd do. He regretted not telling her that he loved her a year ago. When he woke up alone and found her note, those same regrets hit him. He was desperate to tell her now before he couldn't.

His nerves were jumpy, which was never a good sign. That meant trouble was coming or was already here. He hadn't stayed alive all these years as an agent by not trusting his gut. Roman pushed the thoughts of Mina's damaged foot out of his mind. She could take care of herself even with one foot. A little part of him was glad she'd never be in the field again to get hurt or worse—killed. Maybe he shouldn't feel that way, but losing her again was not an option.

Before he could form another thought, he was on the ground and then rolling right back up onto his feet, his body in a fighting stance. Something had knocked him down, and he was ready for the fight. It wasn't until he glanced down that he realized he hadn't been pushed, but rather tripped.

Roman dropped to his knee and rolled the man over, shocked to see Mack out cold on the ground. "Mack," he said, slapping his face a couple of times. When the man didn't come around, he grabbed his radio from his pocket and hit the button. "This is Jacobs. Mack is down."

"What do you mean, Mack is down?" Cal asked when Roman released the button.

"I was running to the cabin when I tripped over his body. He's down. Out cold. I need a med team."

"Why didn't Mina radio for help? They left twenty minutes ago."

"Mina?" Roman asked with his teeth clenched. "She isn't with Mack." Roman released the radio button. That tendril of fear ran up his spine as he glanced around the area. There was no place for her to hide unless she escaped and ran into an empty cabin. He put his hands together and clapped out the rhythm she'd recognize, waiting for a response. When he got none, his heart banged against his ribs. He pulled a flashlight off Mack's belt and shone it around the area. That was when he noticed the grass flattened in one area as it disappeared into the woods. He hit the radio again. "Send help for Mack. Mina is rogue."

There was shouting before light flooded the area. Guys came running out of the lodge while Cal ran full out from the back cabin. He reached Roman in seconds, grabbed his arm and held him in place. "Marlise answered Mina's question, and when they left, I told Mack to get her back to you since I knew you were hot about her leaving. There's no way you missed her on the way out?"

Roman motioned at Mack. "As if she'd just leave him lying here." He pointed at the grass to his right. "Drag marks."

A medical team swarmed Mack, so the two men stepped back. Mack groaned and tried to sit up, but Selina held him down. "Got jumped," he said, his words tight. "Two, maybe three guys. They took Mina."

Roman was running before Mack finished his sentence. They ran into the guest suite, but Mina wasn't waiting for them. The hatch to the bunker was still up, and Cal put his finger to his lips before he pulled his gun. "Hatch was up when I left," Roman whispered. Cal nodded but silently walked to the metal railing protecting the hatch. He swung the gun down the hole several times before he motioned Roman over.

"Mina said she had to talk to Marlise tonight because of something she found. Maybe she left a note."

Cal and Roman climbed down the ladder and

stood in the small computer room. "Everything looks like it did last night," Roman said, more fear spiraling in his gut. "If The Madame has her, we're losing precious time here, Cal!"

Cal jiggled the mouse on the desk, and the screen came to life. A search was open with the picture of two men standing next to each other at a charity event of some sort.

"This mean anything to you?" Cal asked Roman, who jogged over and read the caption.

"Son of a—" Roman ran his hand through his hair to keep from kicking something. "Liam Albrecht and Benjamin Bartos. Liam is the city manager of Red Rye, the office we know stopped her SOS message from going through. Benjamin Bartos is the mayor of a town called Santa Macko in Arizona. Do you think this is what Mina wanted to ask Marlise about?"

Cal grabbed his radio. "One way to find out." He radioed over to the house and asked Selina to find out what Mina needed to know when she was there. While they waited, Roman paced the floor, his mind turning over what little information they had. "What was she thinking leaving without me?" He kicked the chair, sending it spinning across the floor.

"What was I thinking not sending more than one guy with her?" Cal asked, rubbing his forehead. "I was distracted trying to get the nurse to help Marlise."

Roman noticed the fatigue lacing his brother's words and the worry lines creasing his forehead.

"Cal, this isn't your fault. Min knows the risks. She doesn't think she deserves to call herself an agent anymore. That's why she's willing to put her neck on the line to expose The Madame."

"She blames herself for an undercover sting going sideways? That happens all the time, Roman."

"She knows that, too, but this is personal. She feels like she let all those girls down who are trapped by The Madame. Girls like—"

"Marlise." Cal said the name in a tone Roman had never heard come from him before. It was indescribable the pain it held but also the pride.

"She would die to make sure that woman had a chance at life," Roman ground out, his finger pointing toward the cabin beyond the tunnel. "Now I have to be the one to save them both. I cannot lose her again."

Cal squeezed Roman's shoulder. "Does she know you love her?"

The slight shake of his head was enough for Cal to understand. "Then we need to make sure she's around for your lug head to tell her. Tell me what you know about these two guys."

Chapter Seventeen

Where was she? Mina's eyes came open slowly, but she remained still. The air was thick with danger, and it was hard to breathe around the gag in her mouth. She fought the pounding in her head while she gauged the situation. Her body rocked back and forth uncontrollably in the darkness, and she recognized the sensation. She was in a vehicle. It was too dark to see anything, which meant one thing, she was in a trunk or a cargo bay. Her hands were tied behind her back, and her feet were lashed together. Her boot was gone, which would be a real problem if they made her walk anywhere, but thankfully, her feet weren't tied to her hands. She moved her feet forward and back, touching the sides of her cell until she was satisfied that she was indeed in a trunk.

Where were they taking her? The Madame sent her men, but they didn't kill her, which meant maybe they had instructions to bring Mina in alive. She could only hope that was true. It was time to end this game once and for all. She might go down swinging, but at least the other girls would be safe. How, though? How was she going to bring down The Madame by herself with a busted-up foot, no weapon and no way to call for backup?

Mina lowered her head back to the floor and closed her eyes, willing the cobwebs away so she could think clearly. Try to escape. The thought came and went quickly. Even if they hadn't reinforced the trunk latch and taillights, dropping out of a vehicle while tied up was a death sentence. She estimated they were doing at least sixty miles an hour, and there was no way she could outrun them if she did get out. Besides, if they were taking her to The Madame, she wanted a chance to confront the woman.

Fat lot of good that'll do you when you're dead, she thought to herself.

She shifted to get more comfortable when something dug into her knee. She nearly yelped but bit it back in time. Her hands were behind her back, and it took some contorting, but she managed to feel around the pocket of her cargo pants.

Her heart pounded with excitement when she realized she still had Cal's tracking phone! They didn't check her for a phone! That would be their first mistake. If she had anything to say about it, it would also be their last.

Holding herself at a funny angle, she managed to get the phone out and check the display when it lit up. It was almost five o'clock, which meant she'd been out for an hour already. She threw up a prayer of desperation and clicked the star button twice. Then she put the phone on sleep. Ready to slip the phone back in her pocket so they wouldn't find it when they stopped, she hesitated. This might be her only chance to tell Roman how she felt about him.

She painstakingly typed out a message with one hand and sent it, then slid the phone back in her pocket. She had to conserve the battery. If they didn't find her before it went dead, she would be, too.

SHE HAD BEEN gone for an hour already, and they were no closer to finding her. Cal had monitored all outgoing flights from the local airstrips, and there weren't any suspicious ones without a flight plan. She had to be in a car headed to meet The Madame. They had no idea what kind of car or where they were taking her, which only served to fill Roman's gut to overflowing. He had to find her.

Stop. Think.

"Cal!" Roman yelled from where he was strapping on tactical gear and preparing to head out with the rest of the team. "We need to talk to Marlise again!"

Roman heard the squeak of Cal's boots on the ladder, and then he was jogging toward him. "Why?"

"She mentioned that after the cops caught on to their operation, they moved the practice dates to hotels. We need to find out what hotels. One of them may be where The Madame always stays when she's in town."

"I doubt they'd take her back to Red Rye. Too risky, Roman."

"Marlise never said the hotels were in Red Rye," he pointed out and then waited for Cal to catch up with him.

"Good poin—"

"What is that sound?" Roman asked with his head tipped to the left.

Cal's eyes widened when he grabbed the front of Roman's shirt. "Where's the phone I gave you before the trip to St. Paul? The tracker has been activated."

Roman wrenched himself out of Cal's hands and practically skipped the ladder altogether to get to the computer room. He pushed papers aside, cussing up a blue streak until the black device came into view.

"I got it!" he yelled as Cal landed on the concrete surefooted. "It has to be her, right?"

Cal grabbed the phone and slid the bar open to reveal a message. "Oh, it's our Mina," he said, turning the phone back to Roman to read the text. "Meet me at the front of the lodge in three minutes. I need to grab the portable tablet to keep tracking her, and then we're moving."

Roman should have said something in response, but he couldn't. All the air had been knocked from him when his eyes rested on the message she'd sent.

Roman, I'm sorry. I didn't want it to end this way. In a car trunk on the highway. The battery has half life. Find me before it dies, or I do too. Just in case, I love you, Jacobs. Wish I had said it sooner. Maybe we wouldn't be here. Find me.

Roman poised his fingers over the keyboard but hesitated. He couldn't risk sending a message and alerting the people who had her about the phone. It was their only link to her. He'd tell her when he found her. He holstered his gun and took a deep breath. He was ready to fight for the woman he loved.

THE CAR HAD slowed and was driving erratically now. Mina suspected they had reached a city, and she had checked the phone a few miles ago to see they'd been on the road almost ninety minutes since she'd sent the text to Roman. It showed that it had been read, but there was no response. She convinced herself he was afraid to send a message and have it buzz in her pocket. As an FBI agent, she knew he'd made the right choice, but as a woman terrified her life was about to end, she was hoping for an *I love you* back.

She snapped her head around when she heard the siren. It was coming at them, and the car slowed, moving to the right. She could not get this lucky, could she? If a cop pulled them over, she'd make a racket in hopes of getting the officer's attention. Best-case scenario, they get the plate if the driver takes off. She hated that her mind went to the worst-case scenario, and that was the cop getting shot.

She blew out a breath when the siren whizzed past them on its way to a different emergency. Mina estimated it was ten minutes later when the car slowed to a crawl and then came to a stop altogether. She shifted, knowing the time was coming for them to open the trunk. She didn't want them to see the phone, so she rolled onto her side to keep it hidden. Mina could make out the sounds of men's voices just before the trunk popped, blinding her with a bright light. She squinted and blinked until someone leaned in and dimmed the light in her eyes.

"Well, it looks like the special agent is awake. I bet you'd like to stretch your legs for a bit, eh?"

Mina let them manhandle her out of the trunk and set her on her feet. "I can't walk like this. My foot barely works." She had to mutter it around the gag and hoped they understood.

"If you think I'm untying you, you're crazy. Neptune, give me a hand."

She had to work hard not to roll her eyes at their "code" names. Who were these idiots? They wore all black, including black face masks. They looked like a bunch of penny-ante bank robbers, but she wasn't going to egg them on to a beating. They lifted her by her arms, making her shoulders scream in pain, but she kept her face neutral rather than give them the satisfaction of knowing they'd hurt her. They dragged her up a set of stairs in an abandoned warehouse and dumped her onto an old sofa that had been new in the eighties. Neptune yanked her gag down.

"You guys aren't great hosts," she said, shifting to a sitting position, wishing her hands weren't behind her back. "Not even a cocktail?"

The punch to her jaw was quick and unexpected. It knocked her sideways onto the couch. When the stars disappeared from her vision, she sat up again and moved her jaw around a couple of times.

"Is that all you've got?"

Ninja one cocked his fist again, but Neptune caught his arm and held it. "Knock it off, Mercury. They want her alive when they get here. If you don't want to listen to her smart mouth, put the gag back in."

Mina didn't want to be silenced again on the off chance Roman found her before she was dead. "I'll be good," she promised quickly. "Just don't gag me again. I might throw up, and with a gag in my mouth, I could aspirate."

Mercury shrugged his shoulder, ripped the gag up and stuffed it back in her mouth. "You're going to die anyway."

He walked away, and Mina swallowed around the dryness in her throat. She was running out of time and options if Roman didn't get here sooner rather than later. The gag was loose, and she pushed against it with her tongue. She could lower it quickly if she needed to scream, but for now, she'd leave it in place. Better to let them think they'd won. Maybe they had, but she wasn't going down without participating in the fight.

ROMAN HELD THE tablet on his lap. He'd been giving directions over the headset as Cal piloted the helicopter along 35E. It didn't take long for Roman to figure out they were headed for St. Paul. The red dot on the screen stopped, and he held his breath. They were somewhere downtown, but he didn't want to flip into street view yet. It took the tablet too long to switch back if they started moving again.

"They've stopped," Roman said to Cal over the headset. "How far out are we?"

"I've been hanging back, so they don't hear the chopper," he answered. "About ten minutes out from the last coordinates you gave me."

Roman read off the new coordinates. "Get us there, now," he hissed, counting the seconds since the car had moved. "They've been stopped for four minutes."

"Is the tracker moving?"

"Yes, but barely." It was time to hit street view, which he did. When it loaded, his heart sank. "It's a warehouse. I think they're moving her somewhere inside it."

"Give me the address."

Roman rattled it off, his focus never leaving the blinking red dot in the center of the screen. Cal flipped buttons and then motioned above his head for the guys in the back to get ready.

"I'm landing this at the airport. Any closer, and they're going to hear the blades."

"How far out will we be?"

"About a mile the way the crow flies. We'll cover it on foot. There's no other way."

"We may need more firepower."

"We'll call it in."

"Not the FBI," Roman said. "Local guys only. I don't know who we can trust on the team anymore."

"I've got a friend on the force. I've already reached out. When we land, I'll send him the address, and he'll await our assessment."

Roman nodded once as Cal gripped his shoulder for a hot second before the airport came into view. "She's stopped moving."

"Let's hope she's awaiting a meeting with the woman herself. We can scoop up Mina and The Madame and be home by lunchtime."

Roman snorted half a laugh. "It's never that easy with The Madame. But I'm willing to hope you're right."

After Cal set them down, they piled out of the chopper, their tactical gear and automatic rifles at the ready for a fight they hoped didn't materialize. Bullets and dead bodies made for messy final reports when the day was done. It was even harder to explain to the authorities. Cal called his friend and then lined his guys up, Roman directly in front with the tablet.

"We move quickly and quietly. Roman, you're on lead. Anything changes on the tracker, divert, and we'll follow. When we reach the building, we pause and assess."

Everyone nodded, and then Roman led them off to the right, their boots silent in the tall grass, but Roman's heart was pounding so hard he was sure Mina could hear it. He prayed she could because it was the only way he could tell her to hang on.

He pushed the men to move faster, sliding up along the building and holding up his fist, signaling the men behind him to hold. He lifted the infrared scanner to assess the building. It was better than any he'd used in the field. That shouldn't surprise him, considering Cal's ability to get products not even on the market yet. Roman's heart paused in his chest when the scanner picked out a figure in an upstairs room. It had to be her. He called out to her in his head, begging her to hold on. There was another figure in the room, and Roman assessed the first floor before he hustled back to the men awaiting instruction.

"There are three on the main floor inside. A guard at each door makes five. Top floor has two in one room. I know the one figure is Mina. I would guess the other one is The Madame. There are two more outside that room standing guard." The men nodded understanding, but Roman had more information they weren't going to like. "There are two more on the ground, both losing body heat." Everyone knew what that meant. "Watch your six. There will be guns."

Cal was the one to speak next. "We must disarm the guards in silence—no guns or hand-to-hand. Get them from behind and drop them. Roman and I will take out the two guards at the doors simultaneously, leaving the other three guards on the first floor for you four. Whoever is closest takes them down." Everyone nodded, so Cal continued. "Then we'll regroup and rescan the second floor."

Roman used the infrared to scan one more time and gave a thumbs up that nothing had changed. He and Cal set off for the two guarded entry doors while the other men waited to enter the building when those guards were out of commission. Roman wanted to throw the doors open and pound his way through, shooting anyone in his way to Mina, but that wasn't an option. He had to do it right. It was the only way to ensure that she was still alive when they got to her. He swallowed down his terror and crept closer to the guard who had his back to him. How many times had he done this same kind of mission with Min by his side? Countless.

This time, it was on him to save her from certain death. The thought sent a shiver up his spine. It was now or never to be the hero, Roman. Three quick steps had the guard in a headlock and on the ground unconscious. Roman zip-tied him with precision and stuffed a gag in his mouth before he stepped over his flaccid body to the door. The other four men fell in line behind him and Cal, and on three, Roman pulled it open and stepped inside.

Chapter Eighteen

When the door opened, Mina thought she would meet
Liam, Benjamin and The Madame, who wouldn't be
a woman at all but a sitting senator from Maine. She
gave herself a mental shake out and steadied her
breathing. She had remained as still as possible for
the last half an hour, praying it was enough of a signal to Roman that they'd stopped moving.

It would be. Mina believed he was looking for her
because believing anything else meant she would die
at the hands of The Madame this time. Her nerves
were shot, and her foot ached in a way it never had
before. If she got out of this alive, she had a lot of
unpleasant situations to face, but she had to hope
Roman would be there holding her hand through
them all. She believed Mack when he said Roman
loved her. If she didn't, she wasn't going to find the
will to survive this. She might be an FBI agent, but
right now, she was tied up and trapped, which meant
the only emotions coursing through her were those
of a terrified woman who could barely walk, much
less run. Her mind analyzed as much as it could take

in, but it kept coming back with the same answer. She was screwed. Sometimes you had to know when to fold them.

The door opened, and three men walked in, but it was the last one who had her sagging against the couch in relief. "SAC Moore," she said, her voice a mess of relief and respect. "Thank God." Her gaze dashed to the other two men standing next to him. "You got Albrecht and Bartos, good. Did you round up The Madame, too?"

The SAC grabbed a chair and spun it around, straddling it to face her. "I did. I shouldn't be surprised that you recognize these two guys."

"From what Marlise tells me, Liam enjoyed his dates at the Red Rye house a little bit too much." She spat the sentence like filth on her tongue.

"A perk of The Madame," the SAC said. "If he did her bidding, her ladies would do his. It was a win-win."

Mina's gaze tracked the three men, landing on the man who had been her SAC for six years. It wasn't lost on her that he hadn't untied her yet. Also, why was Moore here? If he were here to bust the guys who took her from Cal's, this place would be swarming with the FBI. The rest of the building was silent. The truth slammed into her, and the picture became clear. Disbelieving, she knew there was only one way to find out. She lifted her legs. "How about you untie me, and I'll help you arrest these guys."

"I don't think so."

"You're The Madame," she said, not as a question but as a statement.

The SAC made a so-so hand. "Technically, my wife is The Madame, but you could say we run the business together. You know what they say, if the wife ain't happy, ain't nobody happy."

"So, you run an illegal drug-trafficking business, money-laundering scheme and sex-slave enterprise to keep your wife happy?"

"Well, well, Agent August is well-informed. When this is over, I'll have to find Marlise and have a word with her," he said, practically spitting venom. "I did instruct my men to bring her, too, but once again, their ineptness is astounding. That's what happens when you can't use real agents to get the job done. No matter. I've got you, and you're all I need. Marlise is easy enough to dispatch, and then no one else knows what went on in Red Rye."

"That's not true. Roman knows." Mina was fibbing, but she had to buy herself time before one of the guys with guns came in and dispatched her.

A realization struck Mina. Greg Weiss had been nothing more than a red herring in Red Rye. Mina hated herself for not seeing that and for dedicating so much time to finding a connection between the other two men. Logically there was no way she could have known, but when the trail didn't add up, she should have known it was a ploy.

The SAC motioned the other two men to the door with his head. They left, and it wasn't three seconds after they closed the door that gunshots rang out. She grimaced, but all Moore did was laugh.

"I was done with those two yes men. Let me tell you what, Liam had some serious kinks. The Miss even had a little cleanup with a couple of those girls after he got done with them. At least they were at a hotel, and it couldn't be tied back to Red Rye. Now then, where were we? Oh, yes, Roman Jacobs." The SAC shook his head. "What a lovesick puppy dog he was the past year. Pathetic."

"What does that mean?" she asked, her heart pounding in her chest. They shot the other two men in cold blood, and they'd do the same to her as soon as the SAC tired of their discussion. She had to keep him talking long enough for Roman to find her.

He leaned back, grasping the front of the chair with his hands so he didn't fall. "I was already planning your funeral when he called to tell me you were alive and barely hanging on in the hospital. Of course, by the time I found out what hospital you were at and got a team there, you were gone. I must give you props for that, August. I wasn't expecting you to run in your condition. That took guts."

"Your compliments fall flat when you have assassins at your beck and call."

He shrugged as though her words didn't bite. "Probably true, but don't worry, you won't be facing a firing squad. I'll be the one to dispatch you this time, just to make sure the job gets done right. The last year has been…" he paused and motioned around with his hand. "Trying. I had to listen to my wife complain about you being on the run at home while I listened to Roman whine about you being on the run at work. It was exhausting." He rubbed his temples with his fingers. "Agent Jacobs's desperate desire to find his little woman did offer me an unexpected hand, though."

"His little woman?" she asked with a brow in the air. "I'm his partner. Nothing more."

He waved his hand at her face. "Nice try. As if we're all blind and couldn't see the way you two looked at each other."

"Nothing happened between us," she insisted. It didn't matter to her what he thought, but if it kept him talking, she'd play the game.

"I couldn't care less if it did," he said, his head shaking.

"Partners can't also be lovers. We both knew that."

Her boss shrugged nonchalantly as though they were having a friendly chat rather than working toward her death. "Wouldn't matter to me if you had been. Who am I to judge? Look at me. I'm helping my wife run a criminal enterprise and using my connections at the bureau to do it. What's a little impropriety between friends?"

Apparently, nothing, which Mina never expected from SAC Moore. He was always a by-the-book kind of SAC, at least to their faces.

"That's how the girls' histories and any evidence

they ever existed was wiped away. You used your connections with the bureau."

She could see the gleefulness in his eyes when he leaned toward her. "It's quite easy when you have the right tools."

"Forgive my confusion then, SAC, but if things were going along swimmingly, why did you need to put me undercover in Red Rye?"

He stood and started pacing the length of the room. "I'm so glad you asked, Agent August. We needed someone who could produce an app for us, but first, we needed them to understand the business."

"But I didn't understand the business. I had no idea drugs were involved, though I suspected that money laundering was happening."

He tipped his head back and forth a couple of times. "Okay, that's fair, but you didn't need all the particulars to create the app, only the stuff on the surface that was legal."

"And I handed it to you on a silver platter." She paused and then groaned, her head falling back on the couch.

"It just hit you, right?" he asked, and she glanced up to see him rubbing his hands together.

"The fire happened as soon as I had the app perfected and running smoothly."

"Bingo," he gave her the finger guns. "Thanks for that, by the way. It's a brilliant piece of technology."

"You always intended to kill me once you had the

app, right?" The slight tip of his head answered her question. "How did you plan to get into the back-door of the app where I stored all the evidence if I were dead?"

"That part didn't matter, did it, Agent August? I had no interest in what evidence you gathered or if I could ever access it. We both know none of it was usable in a court of law, no matter the lies I told you to convince you otherwise. That evidence would sit untouched for decades while we ran the operation."

"Which means you didn't keep the app open in case I tried to access it. You kept the app open because you were still using it."

"Both, if that makes you feel better. I prayed you'd try to access it. If you did, Roman would find you, and since we were tagging him, he'd lead us right to you."

"Looks like it worked."

He sat again and leaned forward on the back of the chair. He smiled at Mina with malice she had never seen before. Not even from some of the worst criminals she'd dealt with in the past. This guy was high on power, and he wasn't coming down anytime soon. "Not the exact way I'd hoped, but at the end, when Roman needed some 'mental health' time, I gave it to him." He was throwing air quotes around like a middle-aged woman speaking to a manager. "Then I tagged him and waited. It was only a matter of time. As soon as someone started poking around Marlise, I used her, too. Shame I had to beat up that cute little thing, but I did manage to get you guys to tag her. Always so valiant when it comes to protecting the innocent, aren't you, Agent August?"

"You know you're not going to get away with this, right?" she asked, unable to play nice, knowing the man she had put her trust in was the one to ruin her life.

"Oh, but I am. No one is going to find you. Hard to find someone weighed down with bricks in the Mississippi. I'll go back to work and sit at my desk while Roman searches for you frantically. I'll offer all the resources I can, but eventually, I'll have to have a heart-to-heart with him and tell him it's over. You're lost forever, and he must move on with his life. I have it all planned. It'll be touching."

Mina was about to say something when they heard a noise, and the SAC turned his attention toward the door. She seized the opening she'd been given, and with his back turned to her, she threw herself at him. It didn't matter that she was still tied up. She just wanted the upper hand by dropping his head to the concrete.

They both went down rolling, and Mina fought to get her tied feet to kick out, striking him wherever she could in hopes of keeping him down. His left fist swung out and caught her on the cheek, spinning her head so hard she saw stars, but she couldn't, no, she wouldn't, give him the satisfaction of backing down. He pummeled her head, his mouth spewing obscenities and spit until Mina was nearly unconscious. Her strength almost gone, she struck out one more time—her foot connected with the SAC's jaw and slammed his head to the ground. Mina couldn't celebrate her victory because the impact shattered her glass-like foot.

Her piercing scream of pain filled her ears, and when the door opened, she swore she saw Roman. The darkness tried to take her, but she wouldn't let it. If she did, Roman might let the SAC go thinking he was there to help.

"Mina!" Roman yelled, running through the door and stopping short when he came face-to-face with the SAC, this time with a gun. He'd been hiding it, she knew, because there was no way he was going to leave another attempt at her murder to the men who couldn't get the job done before. He'd been waiting for the perfect time, but now, he was going to get a twofer if Roman didn't have any backup.

"What is going on?" Roman asked, his hands to his sides to show that he had no weapons.

The SAC pushed himself to his feet with a grunt. He swayed visibly from the kick to his head but still managed to hold the gun steady on them. "I should have known the gallant agent would rush in to save his woman at the last minute. Props. I figured I'd tied your hands enough that you wouldn't have a trace on her before it was too late."

Roman took a step to the side, trying to put himself between the SAC and her. "I wouldn't have, but

Special Agent August was smart enough to activate the tracker on her phone."

The gun wavered in his hand, and his face lost what little bit of color was left in it.

Roman smiled a smile he saved for their most sought-after criminals. "I guess your guys forgot to check her for a phone. Classic rookie mistake."

"Don't push me, Jacobs!" the SAC bellowed, flinging the gun around in the air. "There are enough bullets in this gun to dispatch you both multiple times, which is exactly what's going to happen now. I'd planned to let you live. I was looking forward to the months of torture you'd endure looking for your precious Mina, only to find her dead along a riverbank in the spring. Looks like I'll lose out on that funfest this winter. Oh well. I'll have enough to keep me busy trying to clean up the mess August made of Red Rye. If she had just died that night I started the fire, then we wouldn't be here right now. Shame you're going to have to die, too."

"You started the fire?" Roman asked.

Mina saw the exact moment the whole scene came into focus for him.

"You're The Madame?"

Her boss's annoying cackle sent a shiver down her spine. She always hated his laugh. Now she knew why.

"No, but I'm The Madame's better half. It's the little things that matter to the women in our lives,

Jacobs. Imagine if I wasn't here to support my wife's entrepreneurial adventures."

"It's hard to fathom, honestly," Roman said, but she noticed his gaze flick to the door.

Unfortunately, the SAC saw it, too. He got off a shot before a body landed on her, stealing her breath. The weight of him shot a new wave of pain through her.

"Stay down," Roman whispered into her ear.

There was shouting, shooting and chaos for seconds before silence prevailed again.

"Roll call!" Cal yelled out, and all the men responded, including the voice of the man she loved.

"Anyone hit?" Cal asked, but she wasn't paying attention to him. She was staring into the pair of eyes she had seen so many times in her dreams.

"You found me," she whispered, tears in her eyes.

"I'll always find you, Min. Are you hit?"

"I don't think so, but my foot... It's bad, Roman," she said, her voice cracking. "It's bad, isn't it?" She tried to sit up, but he kept her down on the ground, her head cradled by his hand.

"Don't look at it, okay? Police and EMS are on their way. We're going to get you to the hospital."

"The SAC planned this all along," she said, her voice weak from the pain and the terror.

His finger came down on her lips, and he hushed her. "Not another word. You'll need to be debriefed, but you know he's not going to confess."

"He's not going to be breathing if EMS doesn't get

here soon," Cal called over his shoulder from where he knelt next to the man she'd trusted with her life, only to learn he couldn't care less about hers. He was holding pressure on a wound near the SAC's arm while the man was unconscious.

Roman had freed her hands and was rubbing her wrists to get feeling back in them. "I'm going to leave your ankles tied. I don't want to jar that foot, and the other one is keeping it stable. Just concentrate on me, okay, baby?"

"It's bad, Roman. I can't feel my foot."

"It is bad, but I'm here now. We'll get through this together. We'll get you back on your feet and put Moore and his wife behind bars. Together."

"He doesn't need to confess," she said, reaching into the pocket of her pants and pulling out the phone. "It's been recording since I tagged the tracker. I wasn't sure how long the battery would last, but if I had the chance to capture the voice of The Madame, I had to try."

Roman wrapped his hand around her hand, still holding the phone. "That's my girl. An agent until the very end."

"I'm done being an agent now," she whispered, her head falling back into his hand.

He kissed her until she was silent. "I don't care if you ever wear the badge again, Wilhelmina August. You don't have to prove yourself to anyone. We'll get through this together. I hope, when all is said and done, you walk away from the bureau. Hell, I'll follow you."

"Why?" she asked, her hand tucked inside his vest to rest against his chest.

"Department protocol states couples can't be partners. I don't want to work with anyone else."

"Couples? We're not a couple."

"Yet," he whispered, smiling down at her as commotion filled the room. "But I love you, Mina August. I flew all the way here in a helicopter just to tell you that because I refused to tell you by text. You aren't an I-love-you-by-text kind of woman. You're a fancy dinner, roses and the finest champagne kind of I love you. I'll have to give you an IOU on those, but in the meantime, hold on to my love. It will help you get through this."

"You love me?"

"I could say I love you until I'm blue in the face, but sometimes showing is better than telling," he whispered before he captured her lips again.

For the first time since Mina went on the run, she was finally safe from The Madame. She knew from this day forward, the man holding her would be her partner and protector.

Epilogue

"Where are we going?" Mina asked, her laughter filling the late afternoon sky. It was early May, and the weather was warming in Minnesota. It had been a long winter, but she was finally back on her feet and finding joy in life again.

"To my office," Roman said, his arm around her waist and his lips nuzzling her ear. "We have the terms of your employment to discuss."

"My terms of employment? I don't work for you. I work for Secure One."

Right after the New Year, the SAC and his wife were formally indicted for their crimes. They'd stand trial, but with the depth and breadth of the investigation, they were remanded to federal prison until that time. His confession on the audio recording might not be admissible in a court case, and he knew it, but he also knew there was no getting out of the charges of kidnapping and murder.

Mina spent the next two months working with the sex-trafficking team of the FBI. Together, they took statements from the girls in the twelve houses run by The Madame, and helped them find therapy, housing and jobs. She refused to rest until all the girls who wanted help had gotten it.

It helped her work through what she needed to process, too. It reminded her that even though the doctors had to amputate her foot, she could still make a difference in the world. Focusing on the girls made her rehab easier to face and fortified her belief that she could get stronger again. If those women who had gone through hell could find normalcy in life again, so could she.

Though she had a state-of-the-art prosthesis and was active and happy, she didn't have the heart to work for the FBI again. That was probably because the man walking beside her had stolen her heart. When Roman retired from the FBI, she followed suit, and they were hired by Secure One in April. They were still partners, just in a less dangerous way. Mina focused on helping the Secure One team with internet crimes, while Roman taught the team advanced combat techniques and training exercises.

Above all, living and working together made them happy. Mina supposed she could only speak for herself, but she never heard Roman complain about their new arrangement. He woke up every morning kissing her and fell asleep the same way.

From the moment she woke up from surgery after her rescue, she knew he would always be by her side. He was holding her hand, and a tear slipped down his cheek when he had to be the one to tell her the doctors couldn't save her foot. He'd been the one to give them the go-ahead for the amputation, and he begged her not to hate him for that decision.

The truth was, Mina already knew her foot was beyond repair, and the kick to the SAC's face, while satisfying, was the final nail in the coffin for her poor bones. She had slid her hand along his face and wiped his tears, promising that she didn't hate him. He hadn't left her side since. He kept her comfortable and nourished in the early days and motivated her to get up and walk on the hard ones. Now, he kept her up making love half the night, but she wasn't averse to spending every night with him for the rest of her life, so she certainly wasn't complaining.

"I guess we can't discuss your employment then," he said, somewhat downtrodden.

When they reached the lake, most of the Secure One team were walking around sipping on beer bottles and jamming burgers in their mouths.

"We're having a picnic?" she asked, clapping excitedly. "This is great!"

"More like a party, maybe," he said, taking her hand as they approached the group of people milling around.

A woman stepped out of the crowd and ran toward them, grabbing Mina in a hug so tightly that Roman had to grab them to keep them from falling.

"Marlise!" Mina cried with her arms wrapped around the woman. "No one told me you were here!"

"I just got here," she promised, stepping out of the hug to smile at her friend. "I couldn't miss the party, so Cal picked me up in the chopper. I guess I'm staying for the summer," she said on a shrug.

"That's great, Marlise," Mina said, squeezing her friend's hand.

After The Madame was caught, Marlise was moved to a rehab facility that concentrated on physical and emotional healing. She had needed both, but Mina had visited her as often as she could, always with an invitation to return to Secure One when she was ready. Mina had it on good authority that Cal spent a lot of time visiting Marlise, even if he'd claimed he was simply providing protection while she was in the facility. When they raided the other houses around the country, more than one "Miss" had escaped capture, including the one from Red Rye. Until they were all tracked down and brought into custody, any one of them could decide Marlise was a dangerous string to let dangle. The only other strings still dangling from the investigation were the girls in the river. The FBI was trying to tie them to The Madame, but so far, they hadn't offered a big enough carrot to make her talk.

"I'm going to take over the kitchen here at Secure One. I think, anyway. Maybe."

"I hope you do," Mina said with a smile. "Mack is a terrible cook. I told Cal he should offer you the deed to the whole place to get you out here. It looks like he did."

Marlise shook her head shyly. "No, I agreed to try it for a few months to see if I was the right fit for Secure One."

Mina winked at Roman before she turned back to the woman. "I already know you are."

And she didn't just mean in Cal's kitchen.

"I feel safer having you here. Until we find The Miss, you're in danger, Marlise."

"Cal said the same thing, and don't worry. I lived through enough danger to know I don't want to fall into their hands again."

The woman was shaking, so Mina took her hands and squeezed them. "The Secure One team will take care of you until we find her. Then you'll be free to live your life your way."

"I hope so. I also hope I'll figure out what I want to do with my life in the meantime."

"You will, and by the smell of that food, you've already found your calling. Let's eat!"

"Not yet, Agent August," Roman said, pulling her into him and planting a kiss on the top of her head.

"Why not? If Cal's throwing a party, then I'm taking advantage of it."

She noticed his laughter was nervous, and she felt a tremble go through him before he spoke. "Cal's not throwing the party. I am."

"You are?" Mina asked with confusion.

"Right now, it's a picnic. It can't be a party until you answer a question for me."

"Answer a question? What kind of party requires a question to convert it?"

Roman lowered himself to one knee and held up a box. "An engagement party," he said, his voice wavering enough he had to clear his throat.

Mina's hands shook as she brought them to her lips, her gaze drifting to the box when he cracked it open. Shining back at her was a diamond ring in the shape of a star.

"This is the first ring I saw at the jewelers," he whispered, holding up the box in earnest. "I never looked at another ring. This one signified who you are to me. You are my star. You have been since I met you eight years ago today."

Her gasp echoed across the lake now that the picnic had gone silent. "I'd forgotten, but today is the sixth."

"It is, and that's why I waited to ask you this question today. Eight years ago, you agreed to be my partner on the job. I'm hoping today you'll agree to be my life partner. Mina, will you marry me?"

He stood, and she took his face in her hands, planting a kiss on his lips that lasted longer than appropriate when the man was waiting for an answer.

"Was that a yes?"

"Of course, it was a yes. You're my universe, Roman Jacobs. Now put that ring on my finger!"

The team clapped and whistled as Roman slid the ring on her finger and then pulled her close. "And you're my North Star in the night sky, Wilhelmina August. I'll follow you anywhere."

Roman's lips captured hers again, and Mina sighed with contentment. This was the first day of the rest of their lives, and together, they were unstoppable.

* * * * *

Look for more books in Katie Mettner's
Secure One miniseries
coming soon from Harlequin Intrigue!

COMING NEXT MONTH FROM

⬧H HARLEQUIN

INTRIGUE

#2133 SET UP IN THE CITY
A Colt Brothers Investigation • by B.J. Daniels
All hell breaks loose when Willie Colt's extradited felon disappears.
He knows he was set up, and he'll need big-city attorney Ellie Shaffer to
prove it. But nothing—and no one—is what it seems. Soon the dangerous
truth about their connection to the criminal is revealed...

#2134 RESCUED BY THE RANCHER
The Cowboys of Cider Creek • by Barb Han
When rancher Callum Hayes opens his home to Payton Reinert, he knows
she's the only woman who escaped the Masked Monster alive. But how
far will Callum go to protect her from a deranged killer determined that she
won't escape a second time?

#2135 SHOT IN THE DARK
Covert Cowboy Soldiers • by Nicole Helm
Hardened ex-marine Henry Thompson is no babysitter. But when
Jessie Peterson begs for his help locating her rebellious daughter, his
military-rescue instincts kick in. Family treasure, secret doppelgängers and
dogged gunfire are no match for Henry's guard. Jessie, however, is another
story...

#2136 TEXAS BODYGUARD: BRAX
San Antonio Security • by Janie Crouch
When security specialist Brax Patterson gains custody of his nephew, nanny
Tessa Mahoney is a godsend. But his beautiful, secretive employee is more
than she seems...and brings danger to Brax's front door. Is Tessa an innocent
victim of the cartel he's investigating or the one pulling all the strings?

#2137 CATCHING THE CARLING LAKE KILLER
West Investigations • by K.D. Richards
Journalist Simone Jarrett is haunted by the murder she witnessed years
ago. But instead of closure, her return to Carling Lake brings her Sheriff
Lance Webb. With the body count climbing, Lance fears the Card Killer is
back to terrorize the woman who got away.

#2138 RESOLUTE AIM
The Protectors of Boone County, Texas • by Leslie Marshman
Deputy Noah Reed has always been a risk-taker—the exact opposite of his
trigger-shy new partner. But Bree Delgado is no green cop. With a meth ring
exposed and drug runners out for revenge, the bad boy out to make good
will have to trust her to protect his back...and his heart.

**YOU CAN FIND MORE INFORMATION ON UPCOMING HARLEQUIN TITLES,
FREE EXCERPTS AND MORE AT HARLEQUIN.COM.**

HICNM0223

Get 4 FREE REWARDS!

We'll send you 2 FREE Books <u>plus</u> 2 FREE Mystery Gifts.

FREE Value Over $20

Both the **Harlequin Intrigue®** and **Harlequin® Romantic Suspense** series feature compelling novels filled with heart-racing action-packed romance that will keep you on the edge of your seat.

YES! Please send me 2 FREE novels from the Harlequin Intrigue or Harlequin Romantic Suspense series and my 2 FREE gifts (gifts are worth about $10 retail). After receiving them, if I don't wish to receive any more books, I can return the shipping statement marked "cancel." If I don't cancel, I will receive 6 brand-new Harlequin Intrigue Larger-Print books every month and be billed just $6.49 each in the U.S. or $6.99 each in Canada, a savings of at least 13% off the cover price, or 4 brand-new Harlequin Romantic Suspense books every month and be billed just $5.49 each in the U.S. or $6.24 each in Canada, a savings of at least 12% off the cover price. It's quite a bargain! Shipping and handling is just 50¢ per book in the U.S. and $1.25 per book in Canada.* I understand that accepting the 2 free books and gifts places me under no obligation to buy anything. I can always return a shipment and cancel at any time by calling the number below. The free books and gifts are mine to keep no matter what I decide.

Choose one: ☐ **Harlequin Intrigue Larger-Print** (199/399 HDN GRJK)   ☐ **Harlequin Romantic Suspense** (240/340 HDN GRJK)

Name (please print)

Address   Apt. #

City   State/Province   Zip/Postal Code

Email: Please check this box ☐ if you would like to receive newsletters and promotional emails from Harlequin Enterprises ULC and its affiliates. You can unsubscribe anytime.

Mail to the **Harlequin Reader Service:**
IN U.S.A.: P.O. Box 1341, Buffalo, NY 14240-8531
IN CANADA: P.O. Box 603, Fort Erie, Ontario L2A 5X3

Want to try 2 free books from another series? Call 1-800-873-8635 or visit www.ReaderService.com.

*Terms and prices subject to change without notice. Prices do not include sales taxes, which will be charged (if applicable) based on your state or country of residence. Canadian residents will be charged applicable taxes. Offer not valid in Quebec. This offer is limited to one order per household. Books received may not be as shown. Not valid for current subscribers to the Harlequin Intrigue or Harlequin Romantic Suspense series. All orders subject to approval. Credit or debit balances in a customer's account(s) may be offset by any other outstanding balance owed by or to the customer. Please allow 4 to 6 weeks for delivery. Offer available while quantities last.

Your Privacy—Your information is being collected by Harlequin Enterprises ULC, operating as Harlequin Reader Service. For a complete summary of the information we collect, how we use this information and to whom it is disclosed, please visit our privacy notice located at corporate.harlequin.com/privacy-notice. From time to time we may also exchange your personal information with reputable third parties. If you wish to opt out of this sharing of your personal information, please visit readerservice.com/consumerchoice or call 1-800-873-8635. **Notice to California Residents**—Under California law, you have specific rights to control and access your data. For more information on these rights and how to exercise them, visit corporate.harlequin.com/california-privacy.

HIHRS22R3

HARLEQUIN
PLUS

Try the best multimedia subscription service for romance readers like you!

Read, Watch and Play.

Experience the easiest way to get the romance content you crave.

Start your **FREE TRIAL** at
<u>www.harlequinplus.com/freetrial</u>.

HARPLUS0123